The Thin Place

Caroline Smith

Published by Honeybee Books
www.honeybeebooks.co.uk

Copyright © Caroline Smith 2024

The right of Caroline Smith to be identified as the authors of this work has been asserted by her in accordance with the Copyright, Designs and Patents Act 1988.

No part of this book may be reproduced in any form or by any electronic or mechanical means including information storage and retrieval systems without permission in writing from the author.

Disclaimer
This is a work of fiction. Unless otherwise indicated, all the names, characters, businesses, places, events and incidents in this book are either the product of the author's imagination or used in a fictitious manner. Any resemblance to actual persons, living or dead, or actual events is purely coincidental.

Printed in the UK using paper from sustainable sources

ISBN: 978-1-913675-45-5

The Thin Place

Chapter 1
2016

It was about a month after the funeral when Edward called. 'Lucy, my darling girl, how are you?'

'Oh Edward, it's so good to hear from you. I'm glad you're home. Did you and Charles enjoy your holiday?' Lucy felt tears prick her eyes and a huge sense of relief at hearing Edward's voice, as if a weight she'd been carrying around for weeks was being lifted from her shoulders.

'We did my love, although tinged with sadness of course, coming straight after the funeral like that.'

'Yes, Mum's timing always was impeccable,' Lucy said. She could hear the note of cynicism in her own voice.

'And how are you bearing up? And little Daisy, how's she?'

'Oh, you know, taking one day at a time. Daisy's doing okay I think; she's still keen to go to Cornwall with Emily. But we're playing it by ear in case of any last-minute wobbles. To be honest, Edward, I could do with a few days on my own - it's been such a strain and I'm on my knees.'

'Of course it has, my dear. You've been remarkably resilient through it all.' Edward could hear the weariness in Lucy's voice. 'Now, when is it you're going to join Daisy in Cornwall? Remember I need to see you about one of your mother's affairs, as I mentioned at the reading of the will. We can either do it before you go or when you're back, whichever suits you, no pressure at all.'

Lucy had a vague recollection of Edward saying he had something to discuss when the will was read but it was all such an emotional blur, and he and Charles were just off to the south of France, so it had slipped her mind until now. 'I'm going on Wednesday, but once we're back, we haven't anything planned, so we could meet then. Will you be able to come here? I don't think I could face a trip to London straight after Cornwall. So what's it about? You may have told me but if you did, it's lost in the fog of my frazzled brain, sorry.'

Edward hesitated slightly before replying rather elusively. 'It's a bit too complicated to go into now. Yes of course, we'll come to you. It'll be better that way. Shall we say a fortnight on Wednesday? And how're you getting on with probate?'

Lucy groaned. 'It's so tedious but I think I'm getting my head round it. I might want to run some stuff past you though, just to be sure I've covered everything.'

'Of course, my dear. All being well, we'll see you in just over a fortnight but ring anytime you need to, now we're back in the country.'

'Thanks Edward. It is a comfort knowing you're home. See you soon and love to Charles.' Lucy was puzzled about what it was Edward needed to discuss but didn't have the energy to second guess it. She trusted him more than any other human on the planet and vaguely assumed it would be something to her advantage.

Lucy released a heavy sigh and went to find Daisy. It was the beginning of the summer holidays and Daisy had been invited to join her best friend Emily and family on their annual trip to Cornwall. It had seemed like a great idea when it was planned back in the Easter holidays, apart from a rant by Lucy's mother, Suzannah, about how awful Cornwall was and how irresponsible Lucy was, letting Daisy go off with Emily's family. Lucy had let it go at the time, knowing there would likely be another outburst as the holiday approached, but then eight weeks ago Suzannah had died suddenly from a massive stroke and all thoughts of Daisy's trip had vanished. Yet time didn't stand still for the rest of the world, as it had for Lucy. As the summer holidays approached, Chloe, Emily's mum, had gently suggested it might do Daisy good to get away. It was to be the first time Daisy went off without Lucy, apart from a couple of sleepovers, and Lucy worried it might be too soon after Suzannah's death, but Daisy insisted she would be okay and, now the time had come, Lucy knew it was right to let her go. In her fragile state, it would be easy to cling on to Daisy for all the wrong reasons, just as her mother had to her, and Lucy was determined not to let history repeat. It had always been just the three of them and now, aged ten, she needed to be allowed to spread her little wings. Chloe, a teacher at Daisy's school, and Lucy, who worked as a classroom assistant, had been friends since the girls started in year one, so she knew Daisy would be in safe hands.

'Hello love, anything else you want to take?' Daisy was sitting on her bedroom floor studying the contents of her suitcase.

'Well, I've put Little Bear in. Big Bear won't fit.'

'That's a good idea. Take Litle Bear and Big Bear can stay here with me. If you're all finished let's get you into the bath. It'll be an early night so you're ready when Emily picks you up at six tomorrow.' Daisy came and leant against Lucy, wrapping her arms around her waist. 'Mummy, are you sure you'll be all right without me? I won't go if you don't want me to.'

'Oh darling, of course I'll be all right, just as long as you still want to go. And anyway, I'm going to see Ellie and the girls tomorrow, so I'll be fine.'

'Oh okay, that's all right then. Can I have some bubbles in my bath?'

'Yes of course you can,' Lucy laughed, amazed at the candour of children.

***

Lucy sat with her head in her hands and sobbed. Daisy had gone off with Emily and her family with barely a backward glance. Lucy had put on a brave face as she waved them off, but now she was alone and could let herself go, she was in bits. The pent-up grief and anxiety of the last few weeks were released like a crashing wave on the shore and Lucy allowed it to wash over her. After the first few days of disbelief, shock and anguish, she had held it together for Daisy's sake, but now she let the floodgates open. She lay on the sofa and cried herself into an exhausted sleep. She was jolted awake a few hours later when her phone beeped with a message from Chloe.

> At Exeter services. D&E haven't stopped talking since we set off! Think all is going to be fine. I'll txt again when we get to Porthleven. Cx

Lucy smiled but tears pricked her eyes again. She hoisted herself off the sofa and shuffled into the kitchen to make a strong coffee. Dozing during the day wasn't a good idea; she didn't want to tempt any more sleepless nights. As if it wasn't bad enough, it was so much worse in the early hours when there was no hope of returning to sleep, but still ages before it was time to start another day.

While Daisy was away, Lucy planned to sort through Suzannah's things, but now that it came to it, she wondered if it was too soon. Waves of sadness still took her unawares; usually something small would set her off - Suzannah's unfinished book on the coffee table which Lucy hadn't had the heart to move; her tablets, still lurking in a kitchen drawer - and while she could usually get through the day with only a few tears and wanted to move on, it was far harder than she'd imagined, when it came to disposing of her mother's belongings.

Lucy and Suzannah's relationship had been complex. Lucy was an only child, born when Suzannah was in her 40s. When Lucy was less than a year old her father, George, had died suddenly. She had no real memory of him, just a few framed photos scattered around the house of her as a baby, being held by George. Suzannah was deeply affected by the loss of George, and it changed her completely. She became depressed, bitter and emotionally unpredictable. Lucy grew up at the mercy of her mother's alarming mood swings: one minute feeling like she was a nuisance to have around, the next being smothered with stifling affection, more to meet Suzannah's needs than her own. After George's death, Edward, the family solicitor, was persuaded by Susannah to become Lucy's godfather. Although not a religious man, he fulfilled his role as a protective and guiding influence, practically, emotionally and spiritually, and at the same time kept a watchful eye over Suzannah. Without him, it is doubtful whether Suzannah, Lucy and Daisy would have survived as a unit. Over the years, Edward had tried to encourage Suzannah to seek professional help, but she flatly refused counselling, dosing up on a cocktail of anti-depressants, sleeping pills and alcohol instead. 'You keep those quacks away from me, I'll deal with this in my own way,' Lucy could still remember her mother ranting at Edward; he'd had the patience of a saint. She was eventually diagnosed with severe clinical depression and when at her worst, lying in bed unable, or unwilling, to function, Lucy would sit with her for hours, quietly doing her homework in a corner of the bedroom.

Lucy coped with the constant turmoil by avoiding confrontation at all costs; she kept her head down and did as she was told. When Suzannah was having an episode, Lucy looked after herself, as well as her mother. She got herself off to school and made sandwiches for supper, if nothing else had been prepared. Thank goodness for school dinners. Her teenage years were difficult but not in the usual angsty mother and daughter way: she wanted to scream and shout at Susannah, but instead she stifled the rebellion raging inside, frightened of upsetting the fragile status quo, and instead concentrated on getting good grades at school – her means of escape from home and on to university.

She obtained a place at Reading to read psychology. Psychobabble, her mother had called it. 'Why d'you want to do a Micky Mouse course like that, it won't get you anywhere in life,' she'd said bitterly. But Lucy wasn't deterred and even thought it might help her better understand what made Suzannah tick.

Lucy's dream had been to qualify as a clinical psychologist but in her last year at university the worst happened, and she became pregnant. The freedom at being away from home had gone to her head and at the summer ball, at the end of her penultimate year, she'd had a wild night with Danny, a final year economics student (who'd have thought an economics student could even *be* wild, but he was!) By the end of the summer vacation her dreams lay in tatters; while Danny was safely installed in his father's business earning big bucks as an accountant, she was battling morning sickness and exhaustion. It was a mutual decision that neither wanted to commit to the other so in lieu of any practical parenting, Danny paid handsomely with maintenance costs and Edward made sure that the arrangement was legally watertight. Lucy struggled through her final year and completed her studies as Daisy was born.

She'd had no choice but to return home and live with her mother. After bitter recriminations from Suzannah – 'you've wasted your life; how can you ever hope to have a decent career or find a husband' – when Daisy was born, she doted on her granddaughter. She continued to slip into bouts of deep depression which could last for days, but she was less acrimonious, less verbal in her criticism and, over time, she mellowed. Although Lucy could never truly trust her mother, the three of them muddled along, with Lucy continuing to support her as the need arose. Daisy was a happy child and a ray of sunshine in Lucy's life and despite, or maybe because of, the demands of her mother, their bond was unbreakable. Once Daisy started school, Lucy took a job as a teaching assistant and immediately struck up a friendship with Chloe, who had started as a new teacher the same term, while Daisy and Emily became inseparable. Chloe was a huge support to Lucy, understanding how fraught her home life could be, and was always willing to have Daisy when things were difficult with Susannah. She was also determined to find Lucy a partner, although Lucy had promised herself, she wouldn't get into another relationship while Daisy was young; she had enough going on with an unpredictable mother and a growing daughter.

***

Lucy wandered through the house, coffee mug in hand. She caught a glimpse of herself in the hall mirror looking tired and drawn. It was so quiet. No music blaring or tuneless computer sounds coming from Daisy's bedroom. No crockery clinking as Susannah fiddled about in the kitchen, nor the scrunch of the newspaper as she read it in the sitting room. A pall of sadness hung in the air and Lucy opened windows to dispel the gloom. She turned on the radio for some company and her phone rang.

'Hi Lucy. How're you doing Sweetie? Just checking if you still want to join us tonight for a drink.'

'Hi Ellie. I'm okay, I think. Daisy has just gone off to Cornwall with Emily, so I'm feeling a bit adrift to be honest. I'll come along tonight for a bit. It'll do me good, I guess. I just don't want there to be a big fuss.'

Ellie heard the tiredness in Lucy's voice. 'Oh, poor you. It must be so hard. Shall I pick you up, then we can go in together and I can diffuse any inappropriate shows of affection? And if you have a wobble and want to come home early, I'll be happy with that. Can't stay too late anyway, I get so tired with the bump.'

'I remember it well. The last few weeks are so exhausting. If you don't mind picking me up it would be great. I could do with a bit of moral support; I haven't seen some of the others since before Mum died.'

'No probs. See you about seven.'

A slight panic hit Lucy: her first evening out since Suzannah died. She hoped she was ready for it.

***

Lucy tucked herself into a corner of the pub with Ellie next to her. After hugs and muted expressions of sympathy, no one dwelt on Lucy's loss, for which she was grateful. Instead, the six old school friends, who had returned to live locally after university, caught up on news of careers, doing up houses, and who was having the next baby shower. Of the four girls in the group, two were expecting. Lucy felt a surge of regret that she was at a different stage in life from them; had lived a different experience. She stood up. 'Okay, my round. What are we having?' After taking their orders, she stood at the bar waiting for the drinks. She looked over at the group who had been joined by Nathan and Jake, two more of their year. Jake caught her eye and joined her. 'Hi Lucy, long time no see. So sorry to hear about your mum,' and he gave her a hug.

'Hi Jake, thanks.' She was determined not to dissolve into tears, so quickly asked, 'What can I get you and Nathan to drink?'

When they returned to the group, Nathan had taken Lucy's place in the corner, so she and Jake perched on stools on the other side of the table. Nathan was regaling them all with a story about his last trip to New York back in January, when he'd got stuck there in a snow storm for days and missed a stag do in Ibiza. Lucy's phone pinged with another message from Chloe.

> Girls in bed. A few tears from D until we found Little Bear in the case. She remembered Big Bear was looking after you and that seemed to reassure her. They're reading a book together so might be a late one! Won't contact you again unless there's a problem or D wants to chat. Hope you're OK. Cx

Lucy sent a quick reply.

> All good here, thanks Chloe. Kisses to the girls. Lx

She turned to Jake. 'Sorry, needed to get that. So, what've you been up to in the last few years? I heard you moved to Bristol. Is life good there?'

'Ah, you're a bit out of date. I was in Bristol, but I'm in Cornwall now. I had a difficult time about two years ago, split up with my girlfriend. Suffice to say it was messy, so I took myself off to the west country and just sort of stayed.'

'Oh sorry Jake, I had no idea. I'm a bit out of touch I'm afraid. So, what d'you do in Cornwall?'

'Well, much to my parents' disappointment, I do a bit of everything. They think I've turned into a beach bum! I'm an artist but that doesn't pay particularly well so, as a sideline, I teach kayaking and paddleboarding and work at a beach café in the summer months. Most people who live down there have several strings to their bow. It's how the seasonal economy works.'

'Sounds romantic. I seem to recall you were a bit of legend at art. Didn't you do architecture at uni?'

'I did, got as far as Stage 2 and joined a firm in Bristol before it all went tits up. One day I guess I'll have to get back onto the hamster wheel, but for now I'm happy with where I am.'

'My daughter Daisy's in Cornwall at the moment, on holiday with her best friend. They're at a place called Porthleven. Do you know it?'

'I'm just along the coast from there, on the Lizard Peninsular.'

'I've never been, but I'm going in a few days to meet up with Daisy, and then we're taking an Airbnb at a place called Kenneggy. I hear it's very beautiful. We never went to the coast on holiday with Mum; if she was well, we tended to stay with a close family friend and his partner in London, but mostly we stayed home.'

'It is beautiful. I know it sounds clichéd, but it's my spiritual home. I love it.' Lucy noticed Jake colour slightly, as if he was embarrassed at being so open. 'I tell you what, if you've got time, why don't we meet up when you're down? I can show you around.'

'Oh, well, if you don't mind having a ten-year-old in tow, that'd be good, thanks Jake. When are you going back?'

'Tomorrow. Now the holidays are in full swing I need to get back to work. Maybe I can give you and Daisy a kayaking lesson. Let's swap numbers and we can make contact when you're down.'

Suddenly Ellie's voice wafted across the table. 'What've you two got your heads together about? You look very earnest.'

'Just exchanging numbers so we can hitch up in Cornwall. Are you wanting to go Ellie?' Lucy suddenly felt exhausted and hoped Ellie was ready to hit the road.

'Can do. I'm about ready for bed. What a lightweight I am these days! Come on then,' she said, as she gathered up her bag. 'Bye guys, see you next time,' she said to the crowd in general.

'Bye Lucy,' said Jake. 'Good to see you again after so long. Look forward to meeting up in Cornwall.' He smiled at Lucy and for a moment their eyes met. She found it hard to look away and held his gaze ... and felt a stirring inside she hadn't experienced for a very long time.

'Jake's such a sweetie, isn't he?' said Ellie on the drive home. 'I hear he's given up on the rat race, for a bohemian Celtic lifestyle. Lucky him!'

'Yes, seems that way. And he's good company. Not bad looking either!'

'Aye, aye! That's what I like to hear. Time you got back in the saddle again my girl! .... Oh, sorry Lucy, that was insensitive. Probably the last thing on your mind right now.'

'Actually Ells, it was good to forget about real life for a while this evening. Just what I needed. Thanks for the lift and see you again, when I'm back from Cornwall.'

'Pleasure's all mine and remember, if you have a crap day or need a shoulder to cry on just give me a ring and I'll be round. Take care Sweetie.'

Lucy leant across and hugged Ellie and her baby bump, as best she could, over the handbrake.

Chapter 2

1980

'Have you seen that new guy? He's gorgeous!' said Rachel, after taking a gulp of her drink and nearly scalding her mouth. 'Bloody hell, that's hot!'

'Who, Will? Yeah, he's a dish. Apparently, he's from Cornwall. He looks like he's just stepped off a surfboard, doesn't he?' replied Becky. They were on their lunch break, having a coffee and sharing a piece of cake in a café, just off Shaftesbury Avenue.

'Will, nice name. From Cornwall? I think I'll have to offer to show him the sights of the city.'

'Honestly Rach, you're *such* a tart! He's probably left a grieving girlfriend behind and is heartbroken.'

'Well, I'll just have to mend it for him then, won't I? I think I'll ask him along on Friday night. See what he makes of Blitz. It might be a bit much for a country boy!'

'He doesn't really look the clubbing type. He'd probably be happier on a fishing boat! I doubt he'd want to go.'

'Is that a bet?' Rachel was always up for a challenge.

Becky watched Rachel for a moment; she could almost see the cogs whirring, working out her strategy for hooking Will. 'Okay. £1 says you won't be able to get him on a date.'

'A bet it is!'

'Poor bloke, you'll eat him for breakfast. Be gentle with him, won't you?' Becky gathered up her coat and bag. 'Come on, time we were getting back.'

Rachel and Becky met when they joined a bank in London's West End after leaving college, Rachel as a shorthand typist and Becky as a teller. They enjoyed the buzz of working in a busy branch in the heart of London and revelled in the radical social scene of which they were a part. The country was emerging from the infamous 'Winter of Discontent' where widespread strikes had left London's streets littered with uncollected rubbish and hospitals only able to take emergency patients. When Margaret Thatcher brought a vote of no confidence against James Callaghan and became the first female prime minister, she transformed Britain's stagnant economy and re-established the country as a world power. Rachel and Becky were there with the original power dressers in tailored suits and padded shoulders, flashy jewellery and big hair. Punk Rock was fading, New Wave was evolving and clubbing had become a lifestyle. It was into this hedonistic scene that Rachel was determined to introduce Will.

***

Rachel collared Will in the office kitchenette. 'Hi, you're new, aren't you? I'm Rachel.' She gave Will one of her seductive smiles then squeezed past him to reach a mug, brushing up against him in the tiny space.

'Yeah, only been here a couple of weeks. I'm Will.' He tried to move back slightly, which was difficult in the confines of the kitchen, and coloured as he went to shake Rachel's hand.

'How're you finding it? It can be a bit full on when you start. So many people and such a huge building.'

'I'm getting to grips with it. It's once I'm out of the office it's a bit much. I don't really know London at all, so I keep getting lost. I spend most of the time with my head in the A-Z.'

'Where are you from?' Rachel asked, knowing full well he was from the west country.

'From a little place near Penzance in Cornwall. Bit of a contrast.'

'Right. I've never been there, but I'd be happy to show you around here a bit, help you get your bearings. I'm a Londoner born and bred.'

'Um, well yes that would be good, if it's no trouble. I've got a tiny bedsit in Archway, so I know my way in and out of the West End on the underground, but that's about it.'

'I tell you what. A group of us goes clubbing on a Friday night. Why don't you join us? You'd get to meet some people and I can show you some of the best places.'

Will laughed. 'Clubbing? Erm, not sure it's really my thing but I'll give it a try.'

'Don't you have clubs in Cornwall?' asked Rachel, slightly indignantly.

'Yeah 'course we do. There's one just outside Penzance, near the helipad.' Will suddenly felt like he was having to defend himself, then saw the funny side. 'Not quite the West End, eh? To be honest I'm more for driftwood fires on the beach and watching the sunset but, hey, you know what they say, 'When in Rome ….''

Rachel was delightfully puzzled by Will; she'd never met anyone quite like him. So laid back he was almost comatose, and he was such a hunk: medium height, toned body, broad shoulders, dark chocolate-brown hair, and almond shaped deep brown eyes. She felt a bit of a tingle inside. 'Okay then, I'll let you know when and where we're meeting up when Simon's arranged it. See you around,' and she went back to her office with her mug of tea.

Will watched her walk down the corridor. She's a stunner, he thought, and realised his spirits had sunk slightly at the mention of Simon. Of course she's got a boyfriend; looking that good she's bound to have, she was just being friendly, but I may as well go along for the ride. He gave a contented sigh and wandered back to his office.

Will had left his home county of Cornwall to pursue a career in banking. It's not what he would have chosen for himself; his dream was to be a fisherman, but his father persuaded him to follow in his footsteps and join the historic Cornish bank, originally Bolitho Sons & Co. Now merged with a larger national bank, Will had the opportunity to move to a London branch. He knew if he stayed in Cornwall his heart would forever be yearning to join the fishing fleet belonging to another branch of the Carne family. So he'd left, with a plan to return as soon as he'd made his fortune, and buy his own boat.

***

Friday night was a revelation to Will. In Cornwall, a night out meant a smart pair of jeans and a polo shirt (with a tie in your pocket in case one was required to gain entry to a nightclub, or disco as they were still known in the depths of the south west). Here it seemed anything went – preppy, rocker, double denim or a mix of all. Will had opted for a pair of chinos, a white t-shirt with a blue denim shirt over (and a tie in his pocket, just in case!). London fashion for the girls was a world apart – gold lamé jumpsuits, sequined dresses, collared tops, belted waists. Rachel wore metallic leggings, with an oversized off-the-shoulder sweater, sleeves rolled up, and cinched at the waist by a wide belt, showy jewellery and dangerously high heels. Her voluminous auburn hair resembled Farah Fawcett's in Charlie's Angels. Will thought she looked a million dollars.

Will was welcomed into the group with open arms, for novelty value if nothing else. They were intrigued by his life in Cornwall and impressed that he could sail a fishing boat and ride a surfboard. It gave him a certain kudos which was a relief; it could so easily have gone the other way and earned him the country bumpkin label. Rachel introduced him to the crowd, and he felt inexplicably joyful when he met Simon and his wife Becky. Could this mean Rachel is single, he thought? The evening was looking up.

***

Will woke with a banging headache and Rachel's naked body pressed against him. He tried to remember, through the brain fog of a massive hangover, exactly what had happened the night before; all he was sure of was that it was a far cry from any night out in Cornwall. Lying as still as a reclining statue so as not to disturb Rachel, he recalled being in a nightclub, downing far too many weird and wonderful cocktails, dancing like a thing possessed and snogging Rachel as they stumbled and staggered back to his flat in the early hours. As he was trying to drag the remnants of last night's memories to the fore, Rachel stirred. She gave a luxurious stretch, like a cat waking from a sleep in the sunshine, and draped an arm across Will's chest.

'Morning,' she said, with a satisfied smile playing on her lips.

'Morning gorgeous,' he replied, and gently kissed her. 'That was some night.'

'Mmm,' Rachel purred. 'What I can remember of it anyway.'

Will panicked. Had Rachel really wanted to spend the night with him or had he persuaded her when she was in no fit state to say no? There was only one way to find out, 'Rachel, are you okay with what happened last night?'

'Oh Will, you're so sweet. No other bloke has ever asked me that after a drunken night. Oops, that's not to say I jump into bed with every guy I meet.' Rachel gave a little giggle. 'I can add 'gallant' to your list of attractive qualities.'

***

'Told you I'd get him on a date. I think you owe me £1!' Rachel and Becky were in their usual lunchtime haunt, picking over the events of the weekend.

Becky handed over a £1 note. 'And was he worth it?'

'Mmm, you could say that. I didn't leave his place until Sunday morning and we spent most of the weekend in bed!'

'You are such a tart! And how do you always get the best-looking ones? Must be because you're so easy.' Becky was teasing but was secretly concerned for her friend. Rachel was incredibly attractive – slim and petite with a fair complexion, lustrous auburn hair and ice blue eyes – and found it easy to pick up men, which she did with increasing frequency on drunken nights out. Becky worried she was going to get a reputation as an easy lay if she wasn't careful. 'Is he the one then?'

Rachel put her head on one side considering Becky's question, and became pensive. 'You know what Becks, he's certainly different. There's no side to him, he seems truly genuine. No trying to impress with big gestures, just very down to earth.'

'Sounds a bit tame for you then Rach; you usually like them a bit feisty.'

'Mmm, maybe. Perhaps I'm ready for a change.'

Becky was surprised and a little bit hopeful that Will might be a steadying influence on Rachel. 'No doubt you're seeing him again then?'

'You bet. We've already got next weekend planned. I'm showing him some more sights … of *London* Becky, what did you think I meant?' Giggling and arm in arm, the girls left the café and made their way back to the bank.

***

Will could hardly believe he'd been in London over two months. The time had flown and his intention to visit Cornwall after the first month had come to nothing. His job was going well but his love life was even better. All his spare time was spent with Rachel. She was a firecracker, always out for a good time and Will found her lack of inhibition intoxicating. In his eyes she exuded sophistication and confidence, so different from the girls back home. He was besotted. He'd never partied so much, and his sex life had never been so good. He'd become adept at fielding questions from his parents about whether he'd joined a rugby club yet – the truth was he was getting all the sport he needed making love with Rachel.

'Hello Will love, it's Mum. How are you? You haven't called this week.'

Will felt guilty. He knew he was avoiding calling home. 'Hi Mum, yes sorry about that, it's just been full on at the bank.' That was part of the truth but what he really meant was that it was full on with Rachel.

'They do seem to work you hard. I was just wondering if there's any chance you can get away for the bank holiday weekend. I know how important your job is and all, but it's the family barbeque and I'm sure everyone would love to see you and hear how it's going in London.'

'Yeah I'll definitely come down. Leave it with me and I'll make a plan. I may even be able to tag on an extra day. How is everyone anyway?' He felt strangely detached, his life in Cornwall fading like an old memory. How could this have happened so quickly?

'We're alright love, season's nearly under way so it's getting busy. It would be lovely to see you. Are *you* getting on alright?' Will sensed the concern in his mother's voice and it pulled at his heart.

'I'm fine Mum, honestly I'm having a great time and have met some good people who are looking out for me and making me feel at home already.' Will could feel himself blush; the truth was that he was making Rachel feel at home; she was already spending most nights at his place and had all but abandoned the house she shared with a couple of other girls. He couldn't bring himself to tell his mum about their relationship; she'd think it was all far too modern. Maybe when he went home. 'I'll confirm about the weekend when I've checked at work. Look I've got to go. Send my love to Dad and say hi to the rest. I'll see you soon.' He felt a pang of regret as he hung up, but Rachel was all over him and soon all thoughts of Cornwall were forgotten.

Two hours later Will and Rachel were sitting in a bar, Will supping a beer and Rachel cradling a glass of white wine, their desire sated by an afternoon's love making. Will gave a huge yawn.

'Am I wearing you out?' asked Rachel teasingly. 'Too much for you, am I?'

'Yeah, well a trip to Cornwall might be just what I need; a rest from your demands!'

'I don't know what you mean! Perhaps I'll come to Cornwall with you ....' She had a mischievous glint in her eye.

Will felt slightly uneasy. He didn't want to offend Rachel but, in his heart, thought it might be too soon to take her to meet his family. 'Maybe next time. I think they're a bit pissed off that I haven't been back since I moved to London.'

'Don't worry, I wasn't serious. I'll go home too. I don't know how I'd cope in the depths of the west country anyway. The only beaches I've been to are Margate and Benidorm - it's probably not quite the same.'

Suddenly Will felt a longing for Cornwall and, for a moment, wondered if Rachel *would* fit into his slower paced world. He shrugged the thought away and started looking forward to some time back in his homeland.

Chapter 3
2016

During the long drive to Cornwall, Lucy thought through what she'd achieved since Daisy left with Emily. The days had been unexpectedly productive and the task of packing up Suzannah's clothes made easier by reliving the evening spent with her friends, and particularly Jake, and the possibility of seeing him again. She was surprised at how much her mood had lifted, the overwhelming exhaustion of her grief lessening just a little. A few items threatened tears again. At the back of the wardrobe, on a high shelf, she'd found a box containing baby clothes, wrapped carefully in tissue paper: *Babygro's*, cardigans and booties. She placed the box on the bed and lay out the little clothes. Two small black and white photos of a tiny baby lying in a pram were tucked inside the garments. Lucy studied them, touched that Suzannah had kept these items, just as she, Lucy, had a collection of Daisy's 'first' things – the tiny hospital label, her first dummy, her first shoes, her first lost tooth and a lock of her hair. She felt a pang of regret at the realisation that there must have been a softer, more sentimental, side to her mother - one she had never known. Then, as she scrabbled about in the bottom of the wardrobe, pulling out a jumble of shoes and sandals, she stubbed her fingers on something solid right at the back. She pulled it forward, cursing at the weight of it, until it revealed itself to be a safe. It was locked. Puzzled, Luy searched for a key in the usual places – Susannah's jewellery box, knicker drawer and bedside table – but to no avail. She had no energy left for a more extensive search, so gave up and decided to leave it for another day, wondering what Susannah could possibly have kept locked away. With a sigh, she lined up the first few bags for the charity shop.

Lucy had spent hours rooting out information about Suzannah's finances for probate and filling out forms, with only a couple of calls to Edward for assistance. She hoped there weren't any unknown papers lurking in the safe to cause problems later. She'd searched again for a key without luck and there was no way she could break it open; the lock was unyielding. Maybe when she returned from her holiday...

Feeling generally more positive, Lucy booked a session at the hairdresser. Her hair was a mess and hadn't been done in at least two months. She didn't think she'd want to sit staring in the mirror at her drained and tired face, but after a cut and colour, her dark brown hair had copper highlights and fresh layers and she felt her mood lighten further. At least she'd look reasonable if she saw Jake again, she thought, and caught a slight twinkle in her brown eyes, the distinctive gold flecks catching in the salon lights.

As Lucy's journey continued, her thoughts of home drifted away, and she became aware of the changing scenery around her. Past Bristol she noticed the flatlands of the Somerset Levels before crossing into Devon, where rolling hills rose up around her. After a stop at Exeter services, she continued past the wide estuary of the River Exe, then up Haldon Hill and along the A38 with views across to Dartmoor. On to Plymouth and across the Tamar Bridge into Cornwall. What an amazing landscape! Why have I never been here before, she thought, then remembered Suzannah's opinion of this part of the world.

Eventually, after two more hours on the road, Lucy reached the beautifully converted barn where she and Daisy were to stay. Lucy stepped out of the car and stretched, and that's when she felt the soft, warm, Cornish air caressing her skin. She breathed in the scent of sea and summer and listened to the silence. She felt transported to a different time and place, a place she'd never been but which touched the depths of her being. In that moment she understood what Jake meant about Cornwall being where his soul belonged. What a magical place.

Lucy sent a text to Chloe to let her know she'd arrived and, after unpacking and a much-needed cup of tea, went to sit in the little courtyard garden, awaiting their arrival. She turned her face to the sun and closed her eyes. The only sound to break the silence was the soulful cry of seagulls, such an evocative sound even to Lucy, who had spent no time on the coast. And then the peace was broken by the sound of a car pulling up and doors slamming. In a moment, Daisy was flinging herself at Lucy and the rest of Emily's family followed close behind, with hugs and kisses.

'Is this where we're staying? It's really nice. Look Ems, there's a swing and climbing frame over there, let's go.' And the girls raced off to explore the play equipment on a communal piece of ground shared by the three barns in the complex.

'Well, she's obviously missed me!' said Lucy laughing. 'Hope she hasn't been any trouble.'

'It's been great having her; it's almost easier having two of them as they keep one another occupied,' replied Chloe.

'Yeah, and keeps them out of my way!' piped up Tom, grinning. Tom, Emily's brother, was thirteen and having a ten-year-old sister and her friend hanging around was not good for his image.

'Martin and Tom have been off doing dad/son stuff – surfing, kayaking, walking the coast – while the girls and I have mainly been on the beach. The weather has been amazing this year and looks like it's going to continue for a while yet.'

'Sounds like it's been great - thanks so much for having her. I met up with some of my old school friends the other day and one of them, Jake, lives down here now and gives kayaking lessons somewhere nearby. He thought Daisy and I might like a go. D'you think we'd manage?'

'Yeah, it's easy,' said Tom. 'There were some quite old people out on the water when we went, so I'm sure you'd be okay. Oh no, sorry Lucy, didn't mean to imply ….'

'I'd stop digging that hole before it gets any deeper if I were you, Tom!' said Martin.

After another hour or so of sitting in the sun chatting about what they'd been up to over the last few days, Chloe and the family left. They were staying a few more days in Porthleven, so they arranged to meet for supper at the Harbour Inn the next day.

After they'd gone, Lucy cooked a pizza and some garlic bread for them both (well, they were on holiday!). 'How do you fancy a walk to the sea Daisy? I can't wait to see how far we are from the beach. I think we can walk from here.'

'Do we have to? I wanted to play on my *Nintendo Switch*,' whined Daisy.

'Yes well, I need to stretch my legs. I've been in the car for the best part of the day. Let's go and see where the path to the beach is then you can have some screen time when we get back.'

'Okay, if I must, I must!'

'Yep, in this case I'm afraid you must. Come on, we won't be long.'

They set off through the tiny hamlet and found a track leading down to the coast path. Daisy chatted away about what she and Emily had been doing and then asked 'Mummy, were you alright without me? Did you miss me without Granny there? I didn't really miss Granny because I know she didn't like the sea so wouldn't of wanted –'

'Wouldn't *have*,' Lucy corrected automatically.

Daisy rolled her eyes. 'Urgh!' she groaned, before continuing dramatically. 'As I was saying, she wouldn't HAVE wanted to be here anyway. I did miss you a bit though because I thought how much you would like it here.'

'I was fine darling and managed to start sorting out some of Granny's stuff. You're right, she wouldn't have wanted to come here. I don't know why though; I love it already.' And with that the sea came into view and Lucy gasped. 'Oh my goodness, just look at that!' The early evening sun was shimmering across the glittering water and the light on the cliffs caught a myriad of colours in the strata of the rocks. In the distance, still standing proud, was an old Cornish engine house. 'What a place, I'm so glad we came.' And she thought of Jake again, with a lift of her heart. 'We'll go back now Daisy; I'm feeling exhausted after the drive, but I just had to see the sea. Tomorrow let's walk along the coast path to the beach. I might even have a swim!'

'Oh can we? I've been in with Emily and Chloe and it's great.'

***

Later in the evening, once Daisy had played for a while on her *Nintendo* and then gone off to bed, Lucy sat in the pretty sitting room with a glass of Prosecco. It seemed strange having a drink on her own and she didn't want to get into drowning her sorrows. Instead, she wanted to toast the fact she'd survived the last few horrendous weeks, driven all the way from Kent to the bottom of Cornwall (even the Satnav had worked!), checked herself into the accommodation without any disasters and was, so far, feeling okay. Anxiety was never far from the surface these days, but what she had achieved was a great confidence boost and gave her a glimmer of hope that life could go on and maybe even return to (a new) normal. Who knows, it might even bring some new beginnings, she thought. She marvelled at how Daisy appeared to be taking everything in her stride; it all seemed so much more straightforward to her. How she envied the innocence of childhood.

She thought about texting Jake, but then had a pang of doubt – did he really want to meet up or was he simply being polite; was it just one of those times when you say 'Oh, we must get together again soon' knowing full well you won't? Perhaps she was building him up in her mind because he'd been sweet to her in the pub, and they'd exchanged numbers. Easy to swap numbers when you live at the other end of the country. She was pondering what to do when a text beeped in.

Hi Lucy, have you landed in Cornwall yet? Jake x

Lucy's heart was pounding as she answered.

> Hi Jake, that's funny was just thinking about texting you! Arrived a few hours ago and love the place already! Lx

She was about to remove the kiss after her initial but then thought what the hell, he'd put one after his!

> Great, are you still up for getting together? Say if you'd rather not but it would be great to see you. Jx

'I'd love to' Lucy started texting back and then called Jake's number. 'Hi,' she said, when Jake answered. 'This is better than texting. I'd love to meet up. We're going to explore around here tomorrow, and then meet the friends Daisy was staying with for an evening meal in Porthleven. Other than that, we don't have any plans at all.'

'Porthleven? I'll be there tomorrow. I'm going fishing with a mate of mine and we'll be back late afternoon. We could meet for a drink before you go for supper if you can fit it in.'

'Oh okay, I don't see why not.' Lucy's heart was racing. 'I don't know Porthleven but we're eating at the Harbour Inn.'

'It's right on the harbour, as you might expect, and there are loads of tables outside so we could meet there. Shall we say about 4.30?'

'Sounds like a date,' Lucy blushed, realising what she'd said. 'I mean ….'

Jake laughed. 'Yes it does rather, doesn't it? Sounds good to me!'

Lucy felt that little flutter in her insides again. 'See you tomorrow then. If I'm late it's because I've got lost somewhere in the depths of Cornwall.'

'Bye Lucy, looking forward to it already.'

***

Lucy awoke the next morning with the familiar sinking feeling in her stomach as the weight of her mother's death settled on her. She felt confused for a moment, her surroundings unfamiliar and she nearly panicked, then remembered where she was. Her heart lifted as she climbed out of bed and drew back the curtains to be blinded by the intense morning light streaming in through the window. Two hours later, she and Daisy were tramping along the coast path with a picnic, swimming costumes and towels in their rucksacks.

As they passed the ruin of the engine house, tall chimney still intact, Lucy told Daisy what she knew of Cornish mining history and the part they'd played. 'They were built about 200 years ago to hold the pumping engines used to remove water from the tin mines and to power the lifts, called man engines, used to get the men deep into the ground.'

'Why did they need to do that?' asked Daisy.

'Because that's where the tin was, deep down in the rock, and the men had to go down there and dig it out. Some of the seams of tin, went out under the sea.'

'That sounds horrid. It would be so dark. I wouldn't want to do that.'

'It was a hard life, just like coal mining was in other parts of the country.' They took photos of the engine house and moved on. 'I think that's the path down to the beach, but let's go on a bit further shall we and then come back here for a swim and our lunch?'

'Can't we just go to the beach now?'

'I tell you what, let's get round the next headland and then come back. I want to see if we can see St Michael's Mount.'

'Oh yes, we saw it from the car when we were out one day. Emily said it looked like a fairy castle. Can we go there?'

'I don't see why not, if we've got time another day. Come on.' They trudged on, along narrow paths flanked by blackthorn, with barbs that could take an eye out, and wider grassy stretches with tall wildflowers growing up to granite Cornish hedges, topped with a profusion of thrift. The summer air smelt sweet with the coconutty scent of Gorse, and red poppies danced in amongst the grasses.

'There it is!' called Daisy as they rounded the headland and St

Michael's Mount, a castle set on a rocky tidal island off the coast, appeared in the distance. 'I want to go there, I want to go there!' she shouted, as she danced around in front of Lucy.

'Okay, okay, calm down!' laughed Lucy. 'Did you know you can only walk across at low tide, otherwise you have to take a boat?'

'I want to go on the boat!'

'Well, let's find out tide times and costs first. It will be very busy at this time of year.' They started making their way back along the coast path when Lucy spotted a large country house set above them off the path, across a steep meadow bordered by a hedge of Tamarisk trees, their dusky pink feathery fingers waving gently in the breeze. 'Oh, look over there, there's another castle. See the crenelations on top of the walls? Doesn't it look grand? Shall we go and have a look?' They turned inland and followed a path taking them up to the walls of the gardens surrounding the house. They came across a large wooden gate leading through the crenelated wall on which was written 'PRIVATE – RESIDENTS ONLY'. As Lucy took a few paces back to look up at the building, she felt a strange sense of knowing the place. She was sure she'd seen it before, and a shiver ran down her spine.

'Do you recognise it at all Daisy? It looks sort of familiar to me.'

'No. How could I? We haven't been here before. But I love it and I'm going to call it Cornwall Castle.'

'Okay, good name,' said Lucy distractedly, as she stared at the gate in the wall. Where have I seen it before? Puzzled, and feeling rather unnerved, she continued to stare but nothing was coming to her.

'Can we go back to that beach now? I want to swim and have my picnic.' Daisy started tugging at Lucy's arm. Lucy took a couple of photos on her phone, and they set off back to the beach.

Considering Lucy had never been beaching before, she took to it as one who had been doing it all her life. She had a sudden feeling of freedom, like the seagulls wheeling overhead. The feel of the sun on her body was delicious and the shock of the cold water exhilarating: lying on a towel until she was baking hot and could bear it no longer, then plunging into the water to cool down was invigorating. What a lot I've missed, she thought, and was glad Daisy was still young enough to experience it with the innocence of childhood. They built sandcastles together, finding shells and stones to decorate their handiwork, then, ravenous for their sandwiches at lunch time, ate them with the occasional crunch of sand, washed down with ginger beer. How very *Famous Five*, thought Lucy cheerfully. At last, she could forget about the hell of the last few weeks and gave herself completely to this delightful new experience. The beach was busy with other holidaymakers but that was to be expected in high season and, while Daisy found other children to play with, Lucy sunbathed and read her book as her skin darkened.

'Come on Daisy, time to start back now,' said Lucy eventually. 'It's quite a walk and we've got to get ready to meet Emily later.' They packed up their gear and started the climb off the beach. The promise of seeing Emily meant no moans from Daisy.

***

After showering off sand from the beach and salt from the sea, a generous application of *After Sun* and a change of clothes, Lucy and Daisy made their way to Porthleven. Satnav is a Godsend thought Lucy, as she navigated her way there with no mishaps. They had time to stroll along beside the harbour looking at the galleries and gift shops that lined the cobbled street, before settling at a table outside the Harbour Inn, watching fishing boats bobbing on the water and groups of tourists wandering aimlessly around. Suddenly Lucy felt a gentle tap on her shoulder and turned to see Jake standing behind her. 'Hi Lucy. You found it all right then. And you must be Daisy.' He bent and gave Lucy a peck on the cheek then held out his hand to Daisy. 'Glad to meet you.'

'Hello,' Daisy replied. She studied Jake for a moment, shook his hand briefly and returned to her *Nintendo* game.

'I took the liberty of getting you a pint of what you were drinking the other evening,' said Lucy. 'Hope that's okay.'

'Certainly is, thanks. But I think I owe you one from the other night. Next round on me,' and he sat down next to Lucy. 'So, how's it going? How're you finding Cornwall? Is your accommodation okay?'

Lucy was about to answer when a man walked over, calling Jake's name. 'Jake, mate, you left this on the boat.' He handed Jake his mobile.

'Oh blimey, thanks Mike. I'd've been up shi-, oh sorry, young ladies present. I'd've been in trouble without it! Mike, this is Lucy and her daughter Daisy. Lucy, this is Mike who I've been fishing with today.'

'Hi Mike, good to meet you.'

'Hi, sorry to interrupt your drink. Anyway, have a good time and see you next week Jake.' Mike was about to leave when Daisy piped up, 'You look like Mummy!'

'What? Daisy that's not very polite!' said Lucy, her face colouring.

'Well he does! Come over this side of the table and look. His eyes are like yours and his hair's the same colour!'

'Daisy! Don't be so rude!'

Mike was laughing. 'It's okay, don't worry. I've got one about that age and they speak as they find!'

Lucy felt herself blushing and turned round on her bench to take a better look at Mike. He had thick wavy hair like hers, the same shade of brown (without the copper highlights). Like Lucy he also had unusually shaped eyes: a distinctive oval shape, they were dark brown with flecks of gold.

'Now that you mention it Daisy, there is a bit of a similarity,' said Jake, teasingly.

'Don't be stupid, you two!' said Lucy, laughing now. 'Lots of people have brown hair and brown eyes; in fact, probably half the population!'

'Look, I'd better be getting back to Sarah and the kids, for tea. See you, Bud. Nice to meet you ladies,' and Mike strode off along the harbour, grinning.

'Honestly Daisy, that was really rude ……' but she was back into her game and oblivious to the embarrassment she'd caused Lucy.

'Don't worry Lucy, Mike's a big boy, he can handle it. Anyway, what have you been up to today? You're getting a nice tan already.' Lucy told him about their day, how they'd seen St Michael's Mount from the headland and that Daisy was desperate to visit it.

'You don't want to go in the height of the season, it'll be packed! I tell you what though, how about I ask Mike if he'll take us out on the boat and we can sail past the island, see it from the sea. Might even get a bit of mackerel fishing in.'

Daisy wasn't so engrossed in her game that she didn't hear Jake's suggestion. 'Oh can we Mum, please? It would be so cool!'

'Won't Mike mind?' Lucy asked Jake. 'I'm sure he's got better things to do than take us fishing. And haven't you got to work?'

'Well I can ask him. He owes me a favour, and I took the rash decision to clear my diary for the next few days in the hope of spending some time with you, so leave it with me!'

'Yes!' said Daisy with a fist pump. 'Oh look, there's Emily! Emily, over here!' she shouted, as she stood and waved at her friend with family in tow.

Introductions were made and it turned out Jake and Martin vaguely knew each other, having been at the same junior school, but in different year groups. 'I suppose as we're all from Tunbridge Wells it's not surprising,' said Martin. 'Are you joining us for supper?'

Jake looked at Lucy who shrugged. 'Well if you want to and you haven't got other plans it would be lovely,' she said, blushing and suddenly feeling shy. Chloe gave her a knowing smile and a wink.

'Oh yes have supper with us!' said Daisy. Jake had suddenly

become her new best friend with the promise of a boat trip.

'Go on then, why not. It'll beat a sausage sandwich at home!'

Chapter 4
1980

'Okay, I'll concede it's prettier than Margate, but there's nothing going on. Where are the bars and the amusements? No Dreamland here. And what a trek to get here!' Rachel looked decidedly underwhelmed.

'That's what makes it special, it's so natural, so unspoilt.' Will looked at Rachel and could see she wasn't feeling it as he did, every time he stood on the beach at Loe Bar. He loved the contrast of the place - the powerful waves crashing on the shelving sands, and, behind the beach, separated from the sea by a shingle bar, the serenity of Loe Pool, a freshwater lake.

He wanted to explain to Rachel that this was his thin place – a place where, it is said, the veil between this world and the next is at its thinnest; a place where heaven draws closest to earth – where he felt most at peace and his soul restored. But he felt sure she would mock this ancient belief.

'To be honest, it scares me a bit. It's so wild and untamed.' Rachel said, as she snuggled into Will and he held her close.

'If you think this is wild, wait till you see it in winter,' said Will, nuzzling her neck. 'But if you want the bright lights, I'll take you to Newquay. That's about the best you'll get in these parts. It's got fantastic beaches and a bit of night life too. Hardly the London scene though!' He sighed. 'You can't beat this in my book, I didn't realise how much I'd missed the place. Come on, best be getting back.'

In the end, Rachel had persuaded Will to take her with him to Cornwall for the bank holiday weekend. Her own parents had planned to be away and most of her friends were escaping London for the extended break, and she was curious to see where Will was brought up. So many people had raved about Cornwall so she thought it must be worth visiting, at least once. And it was scenic in an empty, rugged sort of way, but so different from the east coast towns and the Spanish resorts she was more familiar with, where everything was on tap for lazy days on the beach and wild nights out at the clubs and bars. And it had rained non-stop on their journey from London, a fine drizzle that turned everything a depressing shade of grey, which did nothing to improve Rachel's first impression. West country sunshine, Will had called it. It didn't bode well for the family barbeque, thought Rachel.

Will had been nervous about bringing Rachel to Cornwall. Would she love it as he did? How would she get on with his family? And what would they think of her? He'd barely mentioned her to his parents and now here he was bringing her home. He'd had an excruciating conversation with his mother a couple of days before they left London.

'If it's okay with you I'm bringing a friend down for the weekend.'

'Yes of course, the more the merrier, what's his name? Does he work at the bank?'

'He's a she mum, she's called Rachel and, yes, she does work at the bank.'

'Oh, well yes that's fine, I suppose. Is she ….? Are you ….? What I mean is, are you an item?'

'Do you mean are we sleeping together? Well, yes, we are. But don't worry, we're happy to have separate rooms at home.' Will wasn't sure Rachel would be, but he'd cross that bridge later.

'Well, yes. I think that would be best. I mean, we've never met her and what you get up to in London is one thing but ….'

'It's okay mum, I get it. Anyway, you'll love her when you meet her. See you at the weekend.'

***

Will's family welcomed Rachel warmly and she found herself enveloped into a close-knit family where no one took anyone else too seriously. It made for a relaxed and cheerful household. No wonder Will's so laid back, thought Rachel.

Will's mum, Pippa, made a special effort (thought Will) to make Rachel feel welcome. 'It's lovely to meet you and I hope you won't feel too overwhelmed by the brood (referring to Will's younger brother, Dan, and twin sisters, Evie and Grace). They're not a bad bunch really, but it can get a bit rowdy sometimes.'

It was so different from Rachel's own home, where she was the only, and somewhat spoiled, child. She *did* feel a touch out of place in this crowded household, the siblings messing about and teasing one another while she watched on from the sidelines, but Will tried to include her and make her feel at home. The bedroom arrangement was a bit of a surprise to Rachel; having been shown where she was sleeping (a pretty room with sea views), she made her way to Will's. 'Why can't I sleep in here with you?' she hissed, hoping no one was within hearing. 'I don't want to be on my own.'

'You'll be okay,' replied Will. 'Mum and Dad are a bit old fashioned in that way and I have to respect their wishes, after all it's their house.'

'But I want to be with you Will,' Rachel whined. 'I don't like being on my own.'

Will was surprised at Rachel's apparent lack of confidence in her unfamiliar surroundings, so unlike the self-assured 'girl about town' in London. He felt a mix of disappointment and protectiveness towards her and hoped, by the time the weekend was over, she would feel more at home with his family and have found a love for Cornwall. He wasn't convinced.

***

For Will, the weekend passed all too quickly. He'd taken Rachel to Newquay (another drizzly day) where holiday makers tramped the streets in anoraks and the sea was gun metal grey and uninviting. 'This is pretty depressing,' said Rachel. 'Not so much bright lights as a damp squib. Still, no worse than Margate on a wet day I suppose. Just give me some Mediterranean sun!' The day improved when they stopped in a cosy pub on the way back, a blazing fire alight in the grate.

The weekend wasn't a complete wash out and a trip to the beach at Rinsey was planned with Dan, Evie and Grace. Rachel was amazed at how far the family was prepared to walk along the rugged coast, carrying their beaching gear to get to a small cove, which involved a precipitous climb down the cliffs. 'I can't climb down there!' said Rachel, horrified at the steep rockface before her.

'Come on,' said Evie encouragingly, 'I'll help you. It's easy. We come here all the time to get away from the crowds.' She held out her hand to Rachel.

'It's okay Evie, I've got this,' said Will, and he scooped Rachel up into a fireman's lift and carried her over the rocks on to the beach, her squeals echoing around the cove.

'Oh my good grief Will!' she said, as he dumped her unceremoniously on the sand, then saw the laughter on the other siblings' faces and saw the funny side.

'Right, last one into the sea's a sissy!' shouted Dan, as he ran into the water. 'Bloody hell, it's cold!'

Grace raised her eyes heavenward and laughed. 'He always says that! Come on you guys,' and she raced after her brother, closely followed by Evie.

'I think I'll just sunbathe for a bit,' said Rachel. 'It'll be way too cold for me,' and she spread a towel on the small stretch of sand amongst the rocks.

'Come on Rach, it's great once you get used to it,' said Will.

'No it's okay, you go. I'm fine here.'

Will felt a pang of disappointment but wasn't going to miss out on a dip, so gave Rachel a kiss and went to join the family. Rachel watched them splashing about wildly and screaming with delight in the cold water, then confidently swimming further out before racing back to the shore. She felt envious of their obvious bond with one another and their oneness with their surroundings. She lay back and closed her eyes. When, sometime later, she propped herself up on one arm she saw that the tide had retreated to reveal a long stretch of golden sand before her. She had to admit, it was a beautiful spot, and they had the beach to themselves. Pity she couldn't swim, but she wasn't going to admit that to this family who were so at one with the ocean. The others were shivering and rubbing themselves vigorously with towels while comparing their swimming prowess, Dan convinced he was the better swimmer. Rachel felt excluded and wanted to sulk, however she couldn't help but be carried along by the family's good humour in the scramble off the beach; how could such simple pleasures bring them so much joy?

Will sensed Rachel's discomfort at the barbeque on their last evening. He endeavoured to include her in the general merriment of the vast gathering of extended family and friends (the Carne clan was Porthleven born and bred) but everyone was keen to find out how Will was doing in London, so apart from an initial interest in Rachel because she was Will's new girlfriend, they were more focussed on Will's life in the city. Will was just as eager to catch up on what had been going on since he'd left, and the chatter soon turned to the local gossip. 'Are you okay Rach?' he kept asking her, her uneasiness plain to see.

'Yes I'm fine, just not the sort of party I'm used to. I feel like a fish out of water to be honest.'

'Yeah it must be a bit strange for you. Sorry if it's not your thing, but it's kind of a tradition to have a barbeque at ours this weekend.'

Will was again struck by how different she seemed – usually the life and soul of any party, here she appeared to be completely out of her depth. He was about to give her an encouraging hug when Tamsin arrived, long tight curls completely out of control as always, hazel eyes dancing in her sunny face. She caught Will's eye and his heart leapt. 'Will, it's great to see you, how have you been? Enjoying the big bad city?' She gave him a hug and a kiss on each cheek and smiled fondly up at him.

'Tam, good to see you. This is Rachel, my er friend from London. Rach, this is Tam.'

'Hi,' they said simultaneously, each assessing the other. Tamzin recovered first.

'Do you work with Will? Hope he's learning the ropes okay and not getting dazzled by those city lights.'

'Yes, we work together, and I've been showing him the night life. Bit different from down here.'

'I'll bet. The best we can do is a disco in Penzance. Do you know Cornwall? Have you been before?'

'No and no. It's my first visit - bit of a culture shock to be honest. I'm a Londoner through and through.'

'Oh right.' Tamzin gave Will, who was watching the exchange between the girls with slight unease, a puzzled glance. 'Well, I hope you love it as much as we all do. *Most* of us wouldn't be anywhere else, would we Will?' she said teasingly, with a wry grin on her pretty face. 'But I guess we can forgive your *temporary* desertion to the big city to make your fortune and bring it home.'

Now it was Rachel's turn to give Will a questioning look. She was about to comment when Seth, Will's dad, shouted to the crowd in general. 'Okay, grubs up, come and get it!'

'After you, girls,' said Will with relief. 'Get in the queue or it'll be gone. Uncle Jethro's here remember!' Tam laughed, but the remark went over Rachel's head.

Rachel had started drinking heavily once the food was served and was somehow persuaded into a contest with Dan, and a couple of his mates, to see who could down the most pints of cider. As the evening progressed, she lost her inhibitions and started banging on the table and demanding another pint. Then she threw up in the garden behind a hydrangea bush and passed out, face down, on one of the wicker sofas in the conservatory. Will was mortified and his parents' embarrassment was obvious. When they were leaving early the following morning, Pippa and Seth were cool but polite to Rachel, and she did at least have the good grace to apologize.

***

On the long drive back to London, Rachel slept while Will reflected on the ups and downs of the last few days. As they approached Stonehenge, Rachel stirred beside him, stretched and groaned. 'Are we nearly there yet?'

'No, we're just coming up to Stonehenge. I'll pull over for a break soon. Look, the stones are over to your left.'

Rachel watched as they motored past the monument, people milling around with cameras snapping. 'Big aren't they?' she said. 'I wonder how they got there.'

'Ah, the age-old question. Some say they originated in Wales. Long way to move them! Anyway, how are you feeling now? Sobered up yet?'

'Bloody hell, that stuff was strong. I was so sick. And I didn't even win! Why did you let me drink it?'

'Like you'd have listened to me. I know what you're like Rach, once you get started; what's that record you hold, the most Tequilas in one night?'

'Yeah, well you were so busy with your friend Tam, I thought I'd make my own fun.'

'I wasn't *busy* with Tam, we were just catching up.'

'I saw the way she looked at you, she's obviously got a crush on you.'

'Don't be stupid, we've known each other since we were kids.'

'And have you ever been out with her?'

'No, not really. We've just sort of hung about, you know.' Will felt himself colouring.

'Yeah, well there's hanging about and then there's hanging about.'

'Give it a rest, she's just a good friend.'

'Sod you, I'm going back to sleep,' and with that, Rachel slid down in the passenger seat, turned away from Will and closed her eyes.

Will had been irritated with Dan for getting her involved in the drinking game, but then Dan didn't know that once Rachel started drinking, she wasn't going to lose face by being the first to stop. Will was still squirming inside with embarrassment, at the way the evening had ended.

Chapter 5
2016

Jake arrived at the barn at the same time as Emily and her parents. Daisy was to spend the day with Emily, before she and her family returned to Tunbridge Wells the following day, and Jake had invited Lucy to go kayaking with him on the Helford River.

'Haven't you had enough of Daisy?' Lucy asked Chloe, giving her daughter a playful nudge.

'Hey, thanks Mum!' Daisy retorted, giving Lucy a dig back.

'No of course not. Tom is going off with one of the friends he's made so it'll be nice for Emily to have Daisy for company. We thought we'd go to Flambards Theme Park,' replied Chloe.

Lucy hated theme parks so was glad to let Daisy go without her. Daisy had been invited on the kayaking trip with Jake too but once the offer of a day with Emily had been made, it won hands down. Lucy felt slightly guilty that she was looking forward to a day with Jake, without Daisy in tow.

Once Daisy was off with Emily, Jake and Lucy drove to the Helford River in Jake's Land Rover Defender, Lucy stealing glances at him as he drove. Tall with sandy hair, blue eyes and a toned body, she couldn't quite believe a) that he was single, and b) that he seemed to be interested in her! Something was stirring in her that had been dormant for far too long. He looked across at her and smiled, and she melted inside.

'What?' she said.

'Just wondering what you were looking at.'

Lucy threw caution to the wind. 'You of course. I happen to find you very attractive! There, I've said it. Am I being too forward?' she said, fluttering her eyelids and waving her hand in front of her face like a fan, feigning coyness.

'Well, how fortuitous because I think you're bloody gorgeous!' He gave her hand a squeeze, and they both started giggling, eyes blurring with tears of laughter. 'Stop it, or I won't see where I'm driving!'

They were travelling along ridiculously narrow lanes, so Lucy pulled herself together and gripped the edge of her seat as they went around another blind bend. But Jake was used to the local roads, and they arrived with no mishaps. The sun was reflecting off the river, and trees grew right down to the water's edge, houses and boathouses peeping out from the woodland. Boats were dotted along the river on their moorings, halyards clinking in the soft breeze, and narrow creeks could be seen branching off from the main waterway. Although it was busy, it had a stillness and peace all its own, calm and serene. Lucy was so moved by the place, she felt tears prick her eyes.

'You okay Lucy?' said Jake, taking her hand. 'What's wrong?'

'Oh sorry, just one of those moments. It's so beautiful. If only Mum could've seen it. I'm sure she would've loved it.' She wiped her tears away.

'Hey, it's okay. If you need to cry, let it out. It's still early days. You're doing so well.'

'Am I? I think I'm doing okay and then something starts me off again. Sorry.' Lucy found a tissue, blew her nose and pulled herself together.

Jake took Lucy's face in his hands and gently kissed her. 'Come on then, sweetheart. Let's get you kayaking.' Lucy felt weak at the knees as Jake helped her out of the Landie and the moment of melancholy melted away.

After two hours on the water, Lucy had mastered her kayak and they paddled up and down the river, along secret creeks and inlets, with the warm sun toasting their bodies and the gentle breeze rippling the water. Jake pointed out Frenchman's Creek, the inspiration for Daphne Du Maurier's classic novel, one of Lucy's favourite authors. 'So romantic,' she said. They pulled the kayaks up on the opposite bank of the river and watched the comings and goings on the water, Lucy leaning back against Jake as he folded his strong arms around her. She couldn't remember when she'd ever felt so calm.

Eventually it was time to leave the peace and tranquillity. 'Come on Kayak Girl, time we were heading back before the tide drops. Then we'll have time for a drink at the pub.'

Once settled at a table overlooking the river with their drinks, Jake took Lucy's hands in his. 'Today's been great, Lucy. I've really enjoyed being with you. Hope we can spend some more time together before you go home, with Daisy too of course: she's sweet and funny, just like you. That's if you want to; you may want to do your own thing after today. Oh, and I spoke to Mike and he's happy to take us out on the boat the day after tomorrow, weather permitting, if you still want to.'

Lucy liked the feeling of Jake's hands holding hers. 'It's been great, I don't know when I've had such a good time. Does that make me sound sad? I'm realising how tied I was to Mum, always tiptoeing around how she was feeling. Oh my life, that makes me sound really bad. Sad and bad, that just about sums me up!'

'Was your Mum ill for a long time?'

'It was complicated Jake. A long story which I'll keep for another day. I want to carry on enjoying this holiday. And yes, we'd love to spend more time with you. And Daisy would never forgive me if we didn't do the boat trip! Talking of which, I suppose we ought to be getting back.'

'I'll confirm it with Mike then. Come on Sad Bad Girl, drink up and I'll take you home!'

***

Two days later they were on Mike's boat, *Spirit of the Sea*, pounding through the waves off the Cornish coast. It was another fine day, but out on the water was considerably cooler, with a stiff breeze blowing from the west. They wrapped up in fleeces and waterproofs. There was a plethora of fishing paraphernalia on the boat, so Lucy and Daisy were given strict instructions on where to sit to avoid getting tangled in any lines, winches or ropes on the deck. Jake helped them on with life jackets and sat between them while Mike took charge in the wheelhouse. He'd brought his son Freddie with him, who was only six and, Lucy thought, far too young to be out on the water, but she soon realised he was already an old hand at life on board, as he sat with Mike on a tall seat, watching his dad steer the boat through the waves. Lucy had been nervous as they set off, convinced Daisy would be lost overboard, but she calmed down as she got used to the motion of the boat and Jake sat with an arm across each of their shoulders.

Daisy was enthralled by the castle sitting on top of St Michael's Mount and was full of questions about how it was built, when it was built, who lived there and so on, none of which Lucy could answer but promised she would find a book that would tell her the history of the place.

'It's okay, I can Google it,' said Daisy.

Lucy groaned and raised her eyebrows at Jake. 'Yes, you can, but it would be much better to get a book about it, then you can take it home and perhaps take it in to school next term.'

'S'pose,' said Daisy, before being distracted by another boat sailing past them in the other direction.

After looking at the Mount from as near as Mike could safely take the boat, they anchored in the bay and tried their hands at mackerel fishing. Jake and Mike set up the lines and held on to the children while they fished, and Lucy took the opportunity to study Mike again. *Was* there a resemblance? The more she looked the more she thought there could be, but then realised how ridiculous an idea it was. Perhaps I've just met my doppelganger she thought (she didn't even know if one's doppelganger could be a different gender!) and smiled at the thought.

Suddenly there was a squeal from Daisy. 'Ugh, they're flapping about, don't let them get me!' she shrieked, as Jake landed one of the lines with six mackerel thrashing about on it.

Jake and Mike were laughing, and little Freddie said "S'alright, they won't hurt you. Daddy's gonna kill them." Daisy covered her eyes while Mike dispatched the fish. Once she'd recovered herself, she inspected the dead mackerel and was fascinated by their iridescent blue and silver skins. She even dared to touch one before drawing back and cuddling up to Lucy.

'That's supper then,' said Jake. 'How about we barbeque them at your place Lucy?'

'Okay, but you'll have to gut them, I haven't a clue. I do love eating them though!'

'Muuum, that's disgusting!'

'All part of the food chain,' said Mike.

'Tastes nice,' added Freddie.

Daisy wasn't going to be outdone by a six-year-old. 'Well, I might try one,' she said pointedly. As she and Freddie were standing looking at one another, Lucy's heart gave a sudden jolt. The two children had simultaneously rubbed a finger under their noses and in that moment, there was an uncanny, almost familial, likeness. She couldn't pinpoint exactly what it was, but it stirred something deep insider her. The moment was gone in a nanosecond, but it left Lucy reeling.

'You alright Lucy?' asked Jake. 'You look like you've seen a ghost!'

'No I'm fine. Just had a moment, that's all. Are we heading back now?'

Jake, assuming it was something to do with Lucy's grieving, continued stowing the fishing tackle while Mike pulled anchor, and they set off back towards Porthleven.

'Look Mummy, there's Cornwall Castle!' Daisy called, as the house they'd seen the other day on the headland came into view.

'How d'you know that place?' asked Mike abruptly.

'Oh, we don't know it, we just came across it on our walk the other day and Daisy named it Cornwall Castle.'

'But you said you thought you recognised it Mummy, which I said was stupid because we haven't been here before.'

Lucy saw Mike looking at her intently with a deep frown, which she found quite unsettling. 'Yes, silly me, I was getting it muddled with somewhere else,' she said, to diffuse what was suddenly a rather tense atmosphere.

'Easily done,' said Jake cheerily, and Lucy was sure he'd noticed Mike's mood change.

'Daddy, I need a wee,' piped up Freddy, which was a thankful distraction and by the time Mike had helped Freddy pee in a bucket and swill it over the side, the house was behind them, and they headed on to Porthleven.

***

Back at the barn Jake barbequed the mackerel – Mike and Freddie having taken their share of the catch back home for their family supper – and Daisy occupied herself on the play equipment.

'What d'you think that was all about with Mike earlier?' asked Lucy, as she watched Jake deftly turn the fillets.

'Yeah I noticed he was a bit curt for a moment there. No idea why.'

'How d'you know him?'

'We met soon after I moved down here. I joined Helston rugby club where he plays. After I'd been here a while, he was looking at building an extension to his house. He knew I'd done architecture so asked if I'd help him design it, which I did. We've been mates ever since. He's got a huge family with cousins all over the place and great parents, and they sort of adopted me into their fold.' He smiled at memories of the family barbeques and beach picnics he'd attended with his surrogate family. 'Mike's a fisherman; it's the Carne family business, but it doesn't make enough to pay the mortgage, so he co-owns and chefs at one of the restaurants in Porthleven. If anyone can cook fish, Mike can.'

'Well, let's hope you can too! Those mackerel smell fab. Cheers!' and she clinked her glass of chilled Pinot with Jake's, all thoughts of Mike forgotten.

After a delicious supper of mackerel – which Daisy tried to enjoy but struggled with the tiny bones – salad and new potatoes, Daisy went in to play on her *Nintendo* while Jake and Lucy sat on the patio, as the sun started to dip in the sky. It was going to be a stunning sunset.

'I can't believe we've only got one more day here,' said Lucy wistfully. 'I don't think I've ever felt so at home, away from home, if you get what I mean. And, forgive me if I'm being rather forward again,' she said with a chuckle, 'but I'm going to miss you Jake Robinson.'

'Feeling is completely mutual, Lucy Askwith.' Jake leaned into Lucy and their lips came together.

Lucy's insides contracted as she thought of saying goodbye to Jake, with no plan to see him again. She wanted to get to know him better, spend more time with him, but didn't think she could navigate a long-distance relationship with so much else going on in her life. Tears threatened, but Lucy managed to blink them away; she knew there would be plenty of time for them later.

'You know I've got a shift at the café tomorrow, and I'd love you to come to Poldhu to join me, but it'll be manic, and I won't have any time to spend with you and Daisy. I think we'll have to say our goodbyes tonight.'

'That's okay, I understand,' answered Lucy, as brightly as she could, while her heart sank. 'I want to explore the beaches here again, before we go. And we've been lucky to have so much of you these last few days.'

'I could always do with more of you Lucy,' said Jake, as he stared at her intently.

At that moment, Daisy appeared at the door in her pyjamas, yawning her head off. 'Mummy I'm going to bed now. Will you come and tuck me in?'

The spell was broken and Lucy got up. 'Daisy, come here and say goodbye to Jake. We won't see him tomorrow and then we're going home, so you'd better say cheerio now.'

Daisy skipped across to the adults. 'Bye Jake,' she said, looking up at him.

'Bye Daisy. It's been good to meet you and spend some time with you. Hope to see you again one day.'

'Will you take us fishing again?'

'Hope so, if you come to Cornwall again.'

'Can we Mummy?' she said, looking at Lucy hopefully.

'Try and stop us! Right, come on, off to bed. I'll be back in a minute Jake.'

'Bye,' said Daisy again, as she skipped off pulling Lucy along with her.

Once Daisy was settled, Lucy realised there was no point in putting off the goodbyes any longer. She ached to spend an evening up close with Jake but knew she wouldn't be able to relax with Daisy upstairs. And anyway, who knew what would happen with their relationship once she returned to Kent. Not the right time to get in too deep.

Jake was leaning against the wall of the garden, watching as Lucy came towards him and fell into his arms. 'I really don't want to say goodbye,' he said, nuzzling her ear. 'You're a breath of fresh air in my life Lucy. I feel like I'm beginning to, well, feel again when I'm with you. To be honest, I wondered if I'd ever know anything like this again.'

'Me too. Dare I say it, it's been many years since I've even dreamed of finding anyone, and now you come along at probably the most difficult time of my life, *and* happen to live at the other end of the country. Great timing, eh?'

'Well, I'm not in any hurry, lovely Lucy, so we've got all the time in the world. Can we just see how it goes, long distance love?' Jake blushed, as he realised he'd said the 'L' word.

'Well, I've got so much on with mum's stuff to sort out and probate, so I'm going to be up to my neck in it for the next few weeks and then it'll be into another school year.' Lucy shivered in Jake's arms, dreading what lay ahead. She'd been able to put it to the back of her mind these last few days but could feel the weight of grief and responsibility settling upon her again.

'Poor you. It's going to be tough. Look, I'll let you know when I'm next coming home so we can get together. I have to deliver some of my artwork to a gallery on the Pantiles for an exhibition later in August, so will be back soon.'

'That would be great.' Lucy sighed and settled in against Jake. She felt she could stay like that forever.

Eventually they drew apart and walked together to Jake's Land Rover. 'Bye then, sweetheart,' he said, and cupped her face in his hands for one last lingering kiss.

'Bye Jake.' Lucy couldn't hold back the tears any longer. Jake kissed them away as more fell. 'Just go, I'll be okay. Always did hate goodbyes,' she said shakily, laughing and crying at the same time.

He let Lucy go, climbed into the Landie and slowly drove away, waving through the window until she was out of sight.

***

Lucy woke with a heavy heart on the last day of their holiday. She was already missing Jake and could feel her mood slipping back to the dark place she'd known since Suzannah died. She knew she must pull herself together so as not to spoil their final day in Cornwall.

When Daisy came bouncing in five minutes later, asking what they were doing, she made a concerted effort to be cheerful.

'I thought we could go along the coast again and see if we can find another beach to explore, maybe find one with rock pools, see if we can catch a crab or find a star fish.'

'Will we find a real star fish? I'll get my bucket and net,' and with that, she was off.

It was a cooler day with more cloud cover, so Lucy was glad they hadn't planned a day lying on the beach. They walked along the coast path in the direction of Cornwall Castle again, but instead of going over to the house, this time they climbed down to the shore below. There was a small patch of beach, but it was mainly rocky outcrops and rockpools. As Lucy stood looking out to the horizon, she felt a strange sense of melancholy and unease. 'Careful how you go Daisy, I don't want you slipping in.' But Daisy was like a mountain goat scrambling her way to the pools, while Lucy followed more gingerly, imagining what injuries could be sustained if one of them fell.

After an hour or so peering into the seawater pools left by the falling tide, they took stock of what they had collected in Daisy's bucket. A tiny crab and two miniscule fish. 'Hmm, could've done better, I think. Perhaps we weren't looking in the right places.'

'I wish Jake was here, bet he would've found a star fish. He's nice, d'you like him, Mum?'

'Yes I do. It was good of him to spend so much time with us. Glad you like him.' Lucy felt herself colouring and thought how stupid it was to feel self-conscious in front of her own daughter.

'I knew you did!' Daisy gave her mother a surprisingly knowing smile before getting back to the bucket.

'Come on, time we put those creatures back in the water where they belong. Can you tip them in gently?'

'Do I have to? Can't I take them home?'

'No you can't. They wouldn't survive and anyway they need to be back with their families in the pool. You wouldn't like to be plucked from your home and taken away in a bucket, would you?!' Daisy was giggling at the idea of being dropped into a child sized bucket of water and gently emptied hers into the water.

As they climbed the path back to the headland Lucy noticed what looked like a small carved stone set to one side, where the path to the beach met the main coastal path. She stopped to read the inscription which said simply 'MC 1981 – 1983'.

'What's that?' asked Daisy, as she noticed what Lucy was looking at. 'Oh, is it a gravestone? What's it doing here. Shouldn't it be in a church yard? What are the dates on there?'

Lucy explained that they were probably the birth and death dates of a child.

'She wasn't very old, was she?' said Daisy. 'Only two. That's so sad. Why is she buried here?'

'She, or he, won't have been buried here. That wouldn't be allowed. It may be that she lived near here or maybe it was a favourite place and the family wanted to put a stone here to remember her, or him, by.'

'When I die this would be a nice place for you to remember me. Where we went rock pooling together.'

'Oh Daisy, don't say that. Hopefully we've both got a lot more years ahead of us.'

'Well Granny died, didn't she? And so did that little girl, or boy.'

'Yes they did. The thing is, we don't really know when it might happen. Which is why we need to have lots of happy times while we can.'

Daisy didn't reply but took hold of Lucy's hand and they walked companionably together back to the barn.

Chapter 6
1980

'If you love it that much, why did you leave?' Rachel complained, when Will was moaning about the smog of the city compared with the fresh marine air of the Cornish coast.

'You know why I left, and I think I'm entitled to feel a bit homesick once in a while. I'll keep my views to myself in future,' replied Will, ready to walk off in a huff.

'I love it when you get bolshy. Here, let me cheer you up!' said Rachel, as she pulled Will to her and kissed him sensuously. When they pulled apart a few minutes later the spat was forgotten.

Since their return from Cornwall, Rachel and Will's relationship had been something of a rollercoaster. The visit to Will's beloved home county, and Rachel's less than enthusiastic reaction to it, was niggling away at him and he wondered whether it was right to continue being together. It had all been such a whirlwind since he'd arrived in London – was it all going too fast? Was she really the girl for him? Could he be with someone who didn't share his love of Cornwall? Rachel, on the other hand, seemed to sweep the Cornwall trip away in a moment and settled back into their city lifestyle with barely a backward glance. Partying and clubbing were back on the agenda and Will felt powerless to resist her potent nature and persuasive personality. After all, she was a stunner, popular with their crowd and always up for a good time. But somewhere deep within him were nagging doubts and a feeling he was travelling too fast along the wrong road. Maybe I'm just being a stick-in-the-mud, he thought, perhaps I *am* a bit of a country bumpkin after all! I'll give it another couple of months, see how it goes.

***

Rachel leapt out of bed and only just made it to the bathroom before being sick. 'I feel like shit Will,' she groaned, as she stumbled back to bed.

'Not surprised, you look like you had a skinful last night.'

'Oh don't start. Anyway, you're wrong. I was feeling rough before I went out so only had tonic water.' She caught Will's doubtful expression. 'What? I did! Honest! You can check with Becky if you don't believe me!' Rachel had been on a girls' night out and Will had to admit, he'd enjoyed having the place to himself for once. He'd had a long, relaxed phone call with his parents and the twins (Dan was out night fishing with Uncle Jethro), without Rachel hovering nearby, gesticulating at him to hurry up.

Two weeks later, the girls were in their usual lunch-break café, Rachel fighting back the tears. 'What the hell am I going to do Becky? It's just such a disaster, I can't believe it. What will Mum and Dad say? And Will's parents, oh my God, they'll probably disown him! They don't like me anyway.' Rachel had vomited every morning for the past fortnight and, after Becky had persuaded her, had taken a pregnancy test which confirmed she was expecting.

'What does Will say?' replied Becky.

'I think he's scared. Scared of having a baby, scared of how we're going to manage, scared of telling his parents, sometimes I think he's even a bit scared of me!'

'Well, you can be frightening at times!' said Becky, trying to lighten the mood. 'Sorry, only joking. For what it's worth, I think you should tell your Mum and Dad first. Surely, they'll support you?'

'Yeah we're seeing them at the weekend, then Will's going down to Cornwall to tell his parents. He thinks it'll be better if he does it without me – charming! It confirms what they think of me – just because I got a bit squiffy and threw up in their flowerbed! Honestly Becky, all we seem to do now is row.'

'It's probably the shock, and your hormones. Once you've all got used to the idea, it'll be fine.' Becky wasn't as convinced as she sounded.

***

The rollercoaster continued. Painful conversations were had with parents; angry recriminations tempered by Will promising to stand by Rachel and to carve out a lucrative career for himself at the bank. He felt the burden rest heavy on his shoulders, and his dream of returning to Cornwall and a fishing boat, slip further away.

As the weeks raced by, Will became more accepting of an addition to their 'family', but Rachel could see no further than how it would wreck their lifestyle, and she became weepy and miserable. When Will tried to reassure her that it was her hormones she lashed out.

'If you tell me again it's because of my hormones I'll bloody swing for you! It's not that, it's because I don't want a baby, end of. I can't believe I even got pregnant. I was only off the pill for a month and then we used protection, well most of the time anyway. How unlucky am I?' Rachel burst into tears. Will tried to comfort her but she pushed him away. 'It's all right for you. It won't affect you, will it? You'll carry on working when I have to stop, and look at me, I'm starting to look like a beached whale already! It's so unfair!'

Will held his hands up in defence. 'Look, I'm sorry but I can't help it that I'm not the woman here. I'd carry the baby if I could! Come on, we aren't the first couple who have had an unplanned pregnancy. You can go back to work after it's born if that's what you want. Look at Pete and Molly; they've had a baby and they both work and have a good social life. It's not the end of the world.'

'Well it feels like the end of *my* world right at this moment. And Molly's nearly ten years older than me. I mean, we're only twenty; there's so much we wanted to do before getting lumbered with kids.'

'Oh, well, sorry you feel it's being *lumbered*. You never said you felt so strongly about it.' But Will knew in his heart they were far too young to be embarking on family life.

'That's because we never even *discussed* it.'

'Bloody hell Rachel, I don't know what to say. So, what d'you want to do? Don't tell me you want to get rid of it?'

Rachel felt like she'd been slapped in the face by Will's comment, and it stopped her in her tracks. 'No, of course I don't want to get rid of it. How could you even think I'd do that?' Tears were stinging Rachel's eyes.

'Well to be honest, I don't know what you're thinking half the time. It's like living on a bloody precipice and not knowing when you might push me off. Your mood swings are off the scale!'

'Look, I'm sorry, okay? I don't want a baby, but I could never terminate it. What d'you take me for? I'm just angry for not being more careful. I know it's your responsibility too but it's usually me who gets carried away in the moment and throws caution to the wind, isn't it?' Rachel gave Will a sheepish smile and her anger subsided.

Will took Rachel in his arms and kissed her gently. 'I know it's one hell of a shock, but we'll get through it. I mean, it can't be that bad otherwise why would so many people have babies?'

'Because they're randy buggers like me?' Rachel replied, and the mood lightened.

***

Michael William Carne was born on 6th April 1980. Rachel's whole pregnancy had been a cocktail of morning sickness, overwhelming tiredness, swollen ankles and heartburn.

'I'm not cut out for this whole mother earth stuff,' she'd moaned to her mother, Anna. 'Other girls seem to sail through it, blooming through the second trimester and nesting in the third, while I drag myself through each day and just want to be anywhere but stuck at home. I've hated every minute to be honest. I'm just not mother material.'

'Don't be silly love. Wait until the little one's born. It will all change then, I'm sure,' replied Anna, with as much conviction as she could muster. She'd never told her only child about how difficult she'd found motherhood (she was only eighteen herself when she became pregnant); how guilty she'd felt when she didn't immediately form a natural bond with Rachel; the depression she'd plunged into after nights walking the floor with a colicky baby. She hoped Rachel would have an easier time of it. The guilt of Anna's lack of maternal instincts never left her. She knew she'd over-compensated and spoilt Rachel as she grew; the little girl never lacked for anything. As a result, she'd developed into a headstrong and confident young woman used to getting her own way and found it hard to take the knocks that life inevitably delivers.

***

'Will, it's your turn,' mumbled Rachel, as she nudged him awake before turning over and falling back into a deep sleep.

Will groaned and got up. By the time he'd warmed a bottle, Michael's cry was building to fever pitch. 'C'mon little fella, let's get you fed,' he whispered, as he lifted Michael from his cot. He watched in wonder as the baby fed and his heart filled with love for the little man in his arms. If only Rachel felt this, he thought. She'd struggled to bond with her son and excused it by saying Michael was a daddy's boy, even as a tiny baby. She liked the congratulatory comments on what a bonny baby they had produced, the oohs and aahs and the 'isn't he sweet', 'doesn't he look like you' remarks, but she didn't like the hard work, being stuck at home and the curtailment of her freedom. Will tried to be understanding and encouraging in the hope she would take to motherhood as much as he had to being a father, but in the end, she took the minimum amount of maternity leave and returned to work as soon as possible. It broke Will's heart to put Michael in a creche but being back at work seemed to make Rachel happier, which made everyone's life easier, and Will had to admit that Michael thrived in the nursery. Gradually, as Michael grew and Rachel felt less restricted by motherhood, she formed a closer bond with him.

***

'Will, what d'you think about having another baby?' asked Rachel one Saturday morning in bed, in the new two bedroomed house they'd recently moved to (helped by Rachel's parents). Will nearly choked on his cup of tea.

'What? Are you mad? It's hard enough with one and he's barely six months old!'

'The thing is, I'm pregnant again.'

'What? How?'

'How d'you think?'

'But after last time ….. how could you let it happen?'

'Oh yes, because it should be down to me to sort out contraception, shouldn't it? The thing is, I forgot to take my pill a couple of times and I got to thinking, as we've got one why not have another. Get it over with while we're young so we've got time to do our stuff later, before we're too old. To be honest, I didn't really think anything would happen, but here we are.'

'You're priceless! And you didn't think to discuss it with me first? And you have such a lovely way of saying things. *'Get it over with'*. Sounds like you're going to have a wisdom tooth removed.'

'Yes, well, believe me, giving birth is way worse than that! I just thought it might be a good idea.'

'You're a mystery to me Rachel, I don't think I'll ever understand you.' But Will was secretly thrilled. He'd almost accepted they were unlikely to have any more children after Rachel's first pregnancy and her struggle to bond with Michael. He put his tea on the bedside table and took her in his arms.

***

Matthew George Carne was born on 15th September 1981. Rachel had sailed through her second pregnancy without any problems and was convinced this baby would be a girl. She was only slightly disappointed when she had another boy, and Will was overjoyed to see how completely she bonded with Matty. Rachel was, at last, content to be with her babies – she had no time to pine for life at the office with two under two – and joined every mother and baby group going. It gave her a social life of sorts and kept the little ones occupied.

Anna breathed a sigh of relief that her daughter had finally taken to motherhood and was easily persuaded to babysit one Saturday evening a month, to enable Rachel and Will to have a regular night out together. She'd seen the strain in Will through the early months of Michael's life, when Rachel had been so demanding and difficult, until she got what she wanted; a return to work. At times, Anna had wondered if their marriage would stay the course but they got through those tricky months – mainly thanks to Will's calm and undemanding nature – and then went and had another baby. She hated to admit it, but she felt envious, and slightly bitter, that Rachel had been brave enough to have a second baby after struggling so much with the first. Anna wondered, if she'd dared to have another, would it have been a better experience of motherhood and prevented the years of self-reproach? And would she have brought Rachel up to be less self-centred; something it was too late to change now, but which she blamed on herself, for submitting to Rachel's every demand in an attempt to assuage her own guilt?

Rachel lived for her Saturday nights out. She and Will picked up with the old gang and the wild nights out in the West End. Rachel was making up for lost time, like a teenager being let out after a month's grounding, and wanted to prove she hadn't lost her touch as the party queen. She was first on the karaoke machine, last to leave the dance floor, and could out-drink the best of them, downing the most shots and being the first to throw up on the way home.

'What an accolade,' slurred Will, as he stumbled along supporting Rachel. 'My other half wins the prize for downing and regurgitating liquor in the shortest time known to man. You should try for a world record.'

Rachel started giggling and then they were both doubled over with laughter, unable to stay upright, until they sunk down against a wall. Then Rachel threw up again. 'Will, get me home. Please. Get a taxi.'

'Won't let us in a taxi, you smell disgusting! Have to get the tube.'

An hour later they were home. Luckily for them, and the wider public, they'd had a carriage to themselves, and the remaining contents of Rachel's stomach stayed put.

'Be quiet Rach, don't wake your Mum,' said Will as he peeled off her coat and dumped it on the floor in the kitchen. If it wasn't completely ruined it would need an industrial clean. 'Get up to bed and I'll bring you a glass of water or you'll have the mother of a hangover tomorrow.'

'Yes Dr. Carne,' she replied mockingly, as she crawled upstairs on all fours. By the time Will arrived with the water Rachel was out for the count, face down on the bed, fully clothed.

'You'll regret it tomorrow,' he said as he removed her shoes, then collapsed in bed beside her.

Rachel did regret it the next day. Her head felt like it was being pounded by a sledgehammer from the inside out and her tongue felt like cotton wool, but not in a good way. 'Oh why did I do it?' she groaned, as Will carried Matty through to their bedroom, Michael toddling along behind.

'What? Get completely bladdered or have two babies who don't respect a lie in?'

'Both,' said Rachel, as she pulled the duvet over her head.

'Mamma, Mamma, Mamma!' squealed Michael as he tried to climb on the bed, but Rachel burrowed deeper under the covers.

'I tell you what, I'll take them downstairs then, shall I?' Will snapped. He could see he wasn't going to get any help. 'Come on boys, let Mummy get her beauty sleep,' he added sarcastically.

'I want Mamma!' protested Michael, as Will pulled him along and out of the bedroom. 'No, want Mamma!' he persisted, so Will hoisted him up on to his free hip and carried both boys downstairs.

'Morning Will. You've got your hands full. Here, let me take Matty.' Anna was already in the kitchen making coffee. She took Matty and put him in his highchair while Will did the same with Michael.

'Thanks Anna. Were they all right last night?'

'Yes good as gold, not a squeak. Did you have a good time?' She placed a strong black coffee in front of Will and gave the little ones a bottle each.

'Yeah it was a laugh. I think we both had a tad too much to drink.' Will nursed his coffee.

'It looks like Rachel had more than a tad, I've seen the state of her coat! Is she not getting up?' Will shook his head and Anna tutted as she started to prepare *Weetabix* for the boys' breakfast.

'Anna, you don't have to do that. You did your bit last night. Sit down, let me.' Will took over mushing up the wheat biscuits while Anna drank her coffee. Both boys were squirming in their highchairs, waiting impatiently for breakfast. 'Okay, okay it's coming! Here we are.' Anna started spooning the cereal mush into Matty's eager mouth while Will helped Michael master the spoon, to bowl, to mouth action.

'It's becoming a bit of a habit, isn't it?' said Anna pointedly. 'Rachel's inability to get up after you've had a night out. She must've drunk London dry last night! Don't you think she ought to curb it a bit, now she's got the boys?'

'It's okay. I don't mind her sleeping it off. Rather that than have her grouching around all day!' Will gave a weak laugh. 'She'll be up soon.' But he knew she wouldn't. She probably wouldn't surface until mid-afternoon, not even getting up to say goodbye to Anna.

This wasn't the first time Anna had mentioned Rachel's alcohol intake and it started to niggle at Will. So, she drank excessively on nights out and had a banging hangover the next day, but did it matter? True, it annoyed Will that she took it for granted he'd do the childcare, but she did it all week, so it seemed fair enough. Perhaps he'd just have a word, more to placate Anna than himself. It didn't go well.

'Mmm, you smell nice,' said Will, as Rachel snuggled up next to him on the sofa fresh out of the bath and in her PJs. 'Better than eau de Vomit anyway.'

Rachel dug him in the ribs. 'That was quite a night, was I very drunk?'

'Just a tad; your mum thinks you must've emptied every pub in the West End.'

Rachel laughed. 'Mum alright, was she? Did the boys behave for her?'

'Yes and yes. But you could at least get up and say thank you to her once in a while. And she seemed a bit worried about the amount you drank, thinks it doesn't become a respectable young mother!' Will was trying to make light of Anna's concerns.

Rachel bristled. 'How does she even know what I had? Unless you dobbed me in William Carne, which I would point out, it is not your place to do!' Will couldn't tell if Rachel was playing around or getting irritated.

'Of course I didn't dob you in but she saw, and smelt, your coat. It's not a great leap from there ...'

'Bloody hell, she'll start poking her nose in now. You could've got rid of the coat.'

'Well sorry if I didn't know it was incriminating evidence.'

'Oh shut up Will. You have no idea.'

'No idea about what? If you don't tell me, how would I know? I'm not a bloody mind reader.'

'Oh nothing. Just leave it will you?' Rachel turned on the TV.

Will shrugged and let it go; anything for a quiet life.

Chapter 7

2016

Lucy was exhausted when they arrived home. The traffic had been relentless, and the journey had taken over eight hours. As she drove further from Cornwall, she felt a wrench she'd never experienced before. She understood why homesickness was so called; the pain inside made her feel queasy and a heaviness settled upon her. She longed for Jake and for Cornwall.

After some initial chatter from Daisy about the holiday, she'd either played on her *Nintendo* or slept, which left Lucy alone with her thoughts for most of the journey. She tried to process her feelings for Jake: were they more intense than they would otherwise be, because she was in a vulnerable place? She didn't want to fall for him for the wrong reasons. Or was it just a holiday romance? Was that even a thing once you hit thirty and had a child? And was it going anywhere anyway, with Jake being so far away? She was certain he was keen on her, but no declarations of undying love had been made and as the journey wore on, her head wasn't any clearer.

As the west country scenery disappeared in the rear-view mirror, Lucy's thoughts turned to home. A knot of anxiety formed in her stomach, and she inwardly groaned at what lay ahead.

***

Lucy opened the door and stepped inside, and familiar aromas hit her. A faint smell of coffee and woodsmoke in the hall and a hint of her mother's perfume at the bottom of the stairs, were usually what provided the comforting embrace of coming home. But instead of feeling the reassurance of being back, Lucy felt overwhelmed with the responsibility of life ahead, just her and Daisy. She'd been able to forget about the magnitude of her mother's untimely death when in Cornwall, but now she was here, reality hit all over again.

Daisy had gone straight up to her bedroom and came back down cuddling Big Bear. 'Mummy, it's horrid without Granny,' she said, and burst into tears. Lucy gathered her up and they sat on the bottom stair together and wept.

When the tears subsided, they unloaded the car in a gloomy mood. Lucy knew she had to put on a brave face for Daisy's sake. When the first load of washing was in the machine, and they'd eaten a supper of fish fingers, chips and peas from the freezer, Lucy suggested they snuggle up and watch a film. 'Your choice Daisy, and let's have some popcorn while we're watching.' Daisy chose *Frozen*, still one of her favourites, but by the end her eyes were heavy and she was nearly asleep. 'Come on sleepy head, let's get you to bed.' Lucy helped her upstairs and once she was tucked in with Big Bear and Little Bear, she was asleep in no time. Lucy was nearly asleep on the sofa herself when Jake rang. 'Lucy, how are you? Did you get back okay? Was the journey awful? It usually is in the summer!'

Lucy's heart leapt at hearing Jake's voice. 'Oh Jake, it's so good to hear you. The drive was bloody awful to be honest. So much traffic. And we've both had a bit of a wobble coming back to the house. It seems so empty and sad somehow. And after such a fabulous time in Cornwall it has hit hard.'

'You poor love. Wish I was there to give you a big hug. I miss you, Lucy. It was so good while you were here. I don't think it's ever felt so amazing being with anyone. You're kind of sexy and dependable all in one! Am I being too forward Ms Askwith? If I am, I don't care! I don't think I made my feelings clear enough before you left but I'm really rather crazy about you.'

Lucy was starting to giggle. 'Oh I say, Mr Robinson, steady on! You could make a girl blush you know! Although I have to say the sentiment is entirely mutual!'

'Well, I'm glad that's settled then! And the good news is I'm coming home for a couple of days and I'm hoping you'll allow me the pleasure of your company. Once I've delivered my paintings and checked in with the parents, I'll be all yours.'

'Now let me check my diary, see if I'm free......of course I'm free! Nothing but clearing more of Mum's stuff on the cards this end. And entertaining Daisy for the rest of the holidays of course.' Lucy suddenly gave an enormous yawn.

'You sound exhausted. Look, I'll let you get to bed and see you soon. I'll confirm exactly when I'm coming so we can sort something out. Take care of yourself, lovely Lucy.'

'And you Jake, thanks for your call, it's really cheered me up. Sleep tight.' Lucy went up to bed feeling more positive than she had all day.

***

Lucy needed some structure to the depressing task of clearing her mother's belongings, which seemed to be taking forever, and made a plan for the next week. She and Daisy agreed that they would have one day at home so Lucy could continue sorting, and then have a day out together or with friends. It worked well: enjoyable days out and about, compensating for painful days deciding what was to become of Suzannah's possessions. By the end of the week most of Suzannah's personal items were in boxes and bags tagged for the charity shop, auction or tip. Lucy felt heartless and guilty at having completed the task so clinically but knew it was the only way she could manage it. She was very aware that the job had to be finished in the holidays, as there would be no time once term started.

Daisy took it in her stride most of the time; just a few tears at bedtime when she thought of Granny reading her a story, and when she was playing in the garden where Granny would often have been, bent over in the borders pulling up weeds and deadheading flowers. They talked about Daisy's sadness and how best to remember those times with Granny, so the memories weren't lost. Daisy chose one of the books Granny most liked to read to her, *The Wind in the Willows*, and picked some of Granny's favourite wildflowers: oxeye daisies, marigold and cornflowers, which they pressed inside the book. 'I'll keep this forever then I will never forget Granny,' said Daisy proudly, as she closed the book and placed it carefully on her bookshelf.

***

It was the evening before Edward and Charles were due to visit. Lucy had spoken to Edward and he had insisted they bring lunch, which Lucy thought cheerfully would probably be a picnic hamper from *Fortnum & Mason*. Daisy was fast asleep in bed. Lucy was exhausted and emotional after days of going through her mother's things, and even felt a little empty inside now that the task was completed. She fetched a glass of wine from the fridge with the intention of flopping on the sofa and watching something mindless on the television. She didn't have the energy for anything else. She glanced at a photo of Suzannah and George on the sideboard as she passed, and her heart stopped. 'I *knew* it!' she said out loud, 'I *knew* I'd seen it before.' There they were standing in front of the garden gate that led to Cornwall Castle. She picked up the photo and studied it more closely. She was sure it was the same place; the garden wall had the same crenelations, as did the top of the building in the background. Lucy scrolled through the photos on her phone until she found the one she had taken just a few days before. It had to be the same place; the only difference was the lack of a sign saying PRIVATE – RESIDENTS ONLY in the old photo. But it doesn't make any sense, thought Lucy. Mum had never been to Cornwall. She said she hated it and would never go. But then, how did she know she hated it if she'd never experienced it? And from the photo it very much looked as if she had been. Questions were racing around in Lucy's head, and she was desperate to talk to someone. For a moment she thought of waking Daisy, but what good would that do, other than result in a tired and grumpy daughter? Then she thought of ringing Jake, but he wasn't likely to have any answers. Lucy downed her wine, lay back on the sofa in frustration and promptly fell asleep. She awoke in the small hours feeling stiff, dry mouthed and disorientated. She fetched a glass of water from the kitchen and stumbled up to bed.

***

Lucy overslept after her disturbed evening and had no time to dwell on the photo. Daisy had been invited to spend the day with Emily and she was late dropping her off. Edward and Charles were due to arrive in time for coffee and after a quick tidy up, the doorbell rang.

'Edward, Charles, it's so good to see you. Come on in.'

'Lucy, my dear girl,' Charles gushed, as he took her into a great bear hug.

'Ah, there you are my dear,' said Edward, following Charles into the hall, carrying a large wicker basket. 'Let me look at you? How are you? You look tired. Are you eating?' And he pecked Lucy on each cheek before hugging her close.

Edward had been in Lucy's life forever. When George died, Edward had acted in the sale of the building company George owned and, aware of Suzannah's growing mental instability, had kept a close eye on Lucy. Charles and Edward, now in their sixties, had been a couple for as long as Lucy could remember. Charles, the more flamboyant of the two, was white haired with ice blue eyes (helped by tinted contact lenses) and Edward, more reserved, had thick salt and pepper hair and hazel eyes. Both were immaculately dressed in pale chinos and Ralph Lauren polo shirts and made a handsome pair, silver foxes with impeccable style.

'Now Lucy, tell me how you really are?' Edward asked, once they were settled with their coffees. 'I've been so worried about you having to deal with everything on your own while we were away. I hope the firm have been looking after you?' Edward's law firm was dealing with the will and probate and so far, all was going smoothly. Edward had been present at the reading of the will, which was all very straightforward as Lucy was the main beneficiary, with a bequest for Daisy in trust until she came of age.

'Yes, it's all fine. Sally at the office has been so helpful.'

'Well that's good. And how was Cornwall? Did you and Daisy have a good time?'

Lucy told them about how she'd fallen in love with Cornwall, and about Jake. 'I was at school with him, and he turned up at one of our get togethers just before I went to Cornwall. Turns out he lives there now, and we spent some time together.' Lucy couldn't help smiling and felt herself colouring. Charles's romance radar picked it up immediately.

'Oh Lucy, do I sense he's got your heart a fluttering? How wonderful! You so deserve a nice young man!'

'Early days Charles, but he is lovely, and he was great with Daisy. He's an artist and is bringing some of his work to a gallery in The Pantiles any day now. He was brilliant at art at school, but I haven't seen any of his recent work.'

'Didn't he show you his etchings in Cornwall?' said Charles, with a twinkle in his eye. 'Well, we must come and visit the gallery; what d'you say Edward?'

'Definitely,' replied Edward. 'And Lucy, it's so good to know you've met someone. A holiday romance, how exquisite!'

Lucy was laughing now. 'Honestly you two, you're like a pair of old matchmakers!'

'Less of the 'old' if you don't mind! And you didn't seem to need a matchmaker, you managed perfectly well on your own!' grinned Charles.

Talk of Cornwall reminded Lucy of the photo. 'Edward, d'you know if Mum and Dad ever went to Cornwall?' She explained about

Cornwall Castle and the photo. 'I don't get it. It has to be the same place, but Mum always said she hated Cornwall and would never go. It just doesn't make sense.' Lucy fished out her phone and showed Edward the photo she had taken, then fetched the one on the hall table.

'Yes it does look the same. To my knowledge they hadn't been there but perhaps they did before you were born, and she just didn't like it.'

'It was more than that, it was like she had a phobia, a sort of dread of the place.' Lucy sighed and placed the photo and her phone on the table.

Edward hesitated before continuing. 'Now, there is the matter of what I mentioned when we met for the will reading.' He stopped and Lucy noticed he suddenly looked his age, his expression drawn. 'Lucy, this is very difficult, but I think we must just tackle it head on. Let me explain. Some years ago, at a time when your mother was in a very bad phase with her mental illness, she left me with a letter which, she said, was not to be opened until her death. In the event of her death, I was to give the letter to you. If I pre-deceased her, it was to be returned to her. As her mental health improved, I asked many times if she wanted me to keep the letter and she always insisted that she did.'

'Okaaay,' said Lucy slowly, thinking it was a bit odd that her mother should leave her a letter. 'And have you got the letter here?'

'Yes I have.'

Lucy felt a pang of anxiety. 'You make it sound as if it might upset me, Edward. D'you know what's in it?'

'Yes, well no, not exactly but I know what it alludes to.' He looked across at Charles who gave a small shrug and looked down at the floor.

Lucy sensed an atmosphere in the room. 'You're scaring me Edward, what is it?' she asked.

'Look, I don't know what's in the letter, but I do know something of your mother's past. It might be a difficult read.'

'Oh please, not more surprises. First, that photo. Then, when I was clearing Mum's bedroom, I found a safe in the wardrobe, which is locked, with no key to be found anywhere. And why would she leave me a letter?' Lucy felt her lips starting to tremble and knew she was about to cry.

Edward was across the room in a second cradling Lucy in his arms. 'My dear girl, please don't upset yourself. We can leave the letter for now.' Lucy cried in Edwards arms until the wave passed over her.

'No, let's do this,' she said, sniffing loudly. Edward gave her a handkerchief.

Lucy opened the envelope with shaking hands. A key fell on to her lap. 'Well, that solves one mystery,' she said, cynically. She unfolded the letter.

My darling Lucy

If you are reading this letter, it is because I have left this earth before I was brave enough to tell you your story. I knew I must tell you one day, but I was too weak; a coward. Once dear George died, it was the final straw, and I became mentally ill. I am more sorry than you will ever know for what I put you through. I was broken and couldn't fix myself. Please forgive me.

What I am going to tell you will be hard to hear but I hope it will help you to understand who I was and why. I hope too that it may open doors to love for you and Daisy, from others that you should have known. I pray it isn't too late for that.

Lucy, I am your grandmother. Your mother had many problems and couldn't keep you. I was ashamed of her, embarrassed by what others might think, couldn't bear the humiliation, so we moved to a new town where no one knew us, and George and I raised you as our own. But the guilt of what we had done grew like a cancer inside and broke me. And without George I splintered into a million pieces. I was scared: of what we'd done, of what I'd become, of what I'd done to you, of what would happen. As you grew into the beautiful, capable woman and mother that you are, I became scared of your rejection. You and Daisy are all I had, and I couldn't risk losing you.

Know this Lucy, I loved you and Daisy more than you will ever realise. I was just so broken inside I couldn't do love properly.

Forgive me.

Your ever loving grandmother

Suzannah

The key will unlock a safe in the back of my wardrobe. I hope its contents will help you find those who you should have known.

Lucy sat, frozen like a moment in time. The letter lay in her lap. She stared: unseeing, straight ahead, as silent tears fell. Edward sat beside her, Charles across the room and no one moved or spoke. Eventually Lucy passed the letter to Edward.

Edward read the letter and his eyes became moist. 'Oh my poor girl, I'm so sorry Lucy,' he said. He took her hands in his; she didn't pull away.

'How much of this did you know?' she asked in a whisper.

'Lucy, I had no idea. I knew something had gone on before you were born but I believed you were adopted. That's what I thought Suzannah was going to tell you in the letter. When your parents –'

'Grandparents,' interrupted Lucy, in a hurt voice, pulling away from Edward. 'They were my *grandparents*, can you believe it?' She got up from the sofa and started pacing the room.

'Yes, grandparents,' continued Edward gently. 'When they told me they were adopting a child, they alluded to you having had a difficult start in life. And I believe that was true but, no, I didn't know you were their granddaughter.'

Lucy was in turmoil, her head spinning with a multitude of questions and scenarios fighting to make sense. Why did this happen, *what* exactly happened, who is her mother, *where* is her mother, is she still alive, who is her father, are they together, why couldn't they look after her? She stood at the patio doors, looking over the garden at the old wooden Wendy house built by her 'father', and sobbed. She felt Edward's arms come around her and fell into his protective embrace. 'My darling girl, what can I do to make this better? Whatever you want, I will help you in any way I can. You and Daisy mean the world to me and Charles; you're not on your own in this.'

Eventually the tears subsided; Lucy felt numb and exhausted. She wanted to shut out the world, to curl up in a ball and sleep like the dead. She released herself from Edward's arms and slumped down on the sofa with a huge sigh. 'I'm just so tired, I can't think.'

'You're probably in a bit of shock. Why don't we leave you to sleep for a bit and wake you for some lunch later.' Edward saw the look of panic in Lucy's eyes. 'It's alright, we won't go. We'll just potter about here. Come on Charles, let's leave the poor girl to sleep.'

***

Lucy woke with a thumping head and groaned as the morning's revelations tumbled into her consciousness. She heard voices in the kitchen and after a moment's panic remembered Edward and Charles were here. She peeled herself off the sofa and went to seek out painkillers. 'My head's pounding,' she said, as she went into the kitchen, then stopped dead at the sight of Jake talking with Charles. She felt herself colour; even in the midst of the day's chaos she was aware of what a mess she must look – hair in a heap and mascara smudged down her cheeks from swollen eyes. 'Jake, what are you doing here?'

'Hi Lucy, I decided to surprise you but it's obviously a really bad time. I'm so sorry, I was just about to leave.'

Suddenly, there was nothing more Lucy wanted than to be held by Jake. 'Oh no, please don't go,' and she launched herself into his arms. 'It's so good to see you. Oh bloody hell, I'm going to cry again. Did they tell you?' Jake held Lucy as more tears fell. Charles and Edward discreetly melted away.

'Edward explained, yes. I hope that was alright? I can't begin to know how you must be feeling, what an awful time for you.' Jake stroked Lucy's hair while her head rested on his shoulder.

Eventually she pulled away, found a tissue and blew her nose. She rooted out some paracetamol from a kitchen drawer and drank them down with a glass of water. 'Oh my days, what a state. I must pull myself together. I think I've cried more in the last few weeks than in my whole life. Surely there can't be any tears left. And suddenly I'm starving. What's the time?' She knew she was rambling on, adrenaline coursing through her body, nerves shot to pieces.

'About half-one, I think. Edward and Charles have laid out some lunch in the dining room. They were worried they'd have to take it home uneaten, so they'll be pleased you're hungry.'

The four of them ate companionably around the dining room table, a picnic of artisan bread, French cheeses and charcuterie, salads and pickles, all beautifully prepared and presented by *Messrs Fortnum & Mason*. With food inside her and re-hydrated, Lucy started to feel less drained. She watched as Jake chatted easily with Edward and Charles, happy to observe from the sidelines; she had little energy for small talk. When they'd eaten their fill, Charles and Jake started clearing away the lunchtime leftovers, while Edward asked when Daisy was due home and what Lucy wanted to do; did she want to tell her straight away or wait for a while?

'I wish I didn't have to tell her at all but of course I do. I don't want to run the risk of waiting until the *right time*, and then the right time never coming. And hey ho, then history will repeat itself all over again,' she said bitterly. 'God alone knows what it will do to her. She loved her granny so much.'

'I know it will be hard, but it may not be as big for her as it is for you. In effect, she'll just be adding a 'great' to her granny; the *person* she knew won't have changed, so if you put it to her like that, it might not be such a blow. She's still young; you'll have time to help her understand the details as time goes on and you know more yourself. My suggestion would be to keep it simple and not try to over explain.'

'You're so wise Edward. I only wish I could look at it like that but it's my whole life story that's been a lie. I'm so angry with Mum.'

'Of course you are right now, it's to be expected. Now, would you like us to stay with you while you tell Daisy? Just to give you some moral support?'

'Would you? I just don't know how I'll cope if she takes it badly. She should be home soon, Chloe's dropping her off.'

Jake and Charles appeared from the kitchen. 'All cleared up,' said Jake.

'Yes, dishwasher stacked and leftovers in the fridge,' added Charles.

'Charles darling, we're going to stay for a bit longer and see Daisy when she gets home.' Edward gave Charles a knowing look.

'Of course, it will be lovely to see Daisy.'

Jake was relieved that Lucy wouldn't be alone and decided to carry on to his parents' house while she was in the safe hands of her oldest and dearest friends. He didn't want to be an extra distraction when Daisy came home and was told the news of her granny.

Lucy felt a moment of panic. 'Can you come tomorrow, Jake? It's my turn to have Emily here and if Daisy is okay, I think it will be good to stick to the plan. Would you be able to be here when I open that bloody safe? I just can't cope with it on my own.' She handed Jake the key. 'In fact, will you take this so I'm not tempted to open it today, I can't take any more of my mother's revelations from the grave. We'll do it tomorrow.'

'Yes of course, if you're sure you want me here. *And* you're entrusting me with the key? I'm actually rather flattered, if that's not an inappropriate turn of phrase given the circumstances. Sorry, not trying to make light ….'

Lucy laughed weakly. 'I think a bit of light relief is what we need right now. It's all so sad and depressing. Just don't lose the key!'

***

Daisy came bouncing in full of her day with Emily. 'We went swimming at Tonbridge, in the outdoor pool, and then had a picnic in the park. It was great. Edward, you swim through this little tunnel from the indoor to the outdoor pool. It's so cool.'

'I'm glad you had such a good day. You'll have to take me to the pool one day.'

Lucy and Charles appeared from the kitchen carrying a tray of tea and biscuits and a glass of squash for Daisy.

'Hi Charles,' said Daisy taking the glass of squash and sitting next to him on the sofa.

'Hello Daisy, my dear girl; goodness you've grown again!'

Daisy groaned. 'You *always* say that!' but she was starting to giggle.

'Do I? Well that's because every time I see you, you *have* grown. What's a chap to do?'

Daisy was laughing now; she always found Charles comical, with his old-fashioned turn of phrase.

Once everyone was refreshed with drinks and biscuits, a quiet descended and a sort of unspoken signal passed between Lucy, Edward and Charles.

'Daisy, Edward came today to tell me something about Granny that I didn't know before. It's a big piece of news so I wanted to tell you too.' Lucy glanced at Edward who gave her an encouraging nod.

'The thing is, Granny was actually your Great Granny and she was *my* Granny. And that's because I never had a mummy, so Granny became my mummy while I was growing up. Do you understand?'

Daisy was sitting very still, looking down and frowning hard. No one spoke. After a moment she raised her head. 'I think so. It's nice I had a Great Granny; there's not many in my class with great grandparents. I know that because we did family trees last term. Oh, mine will be wrong now, I wonder if I can do it again when we go back to school. But it's sad you didn't have a mummy. Didn't you mind not having a mummy?'

'Well no, not really, because I thought Granny was my mummy. She was going to tell me, once I grew up, but she didn't manage to before she died.'

'Did your mummy die too? Is that why Granny was your mummy?'

'We don't know that so it's something I hope I will find out one day.'

'Okay.' Daisy was thoughtful for a moment then asked if she could have another biscuit. It seemed she had taken in enough information for now and Lucy decided to leave it there and give her time to process what she'd been told. She didn't doubt there would be more questions later, but she wanted to be led by Daisy and not push it.

'Daisy, will you show me the Wendy house? I don't believe you can still fit in there, can you?' said Charles, with a mischievous twinkle in his eye.

'I can! I haven't grown *that* much! Come on, I'll show you!' and she pulled Charles off the sofa and into the garden.

Lucy gave a huge sigh. 'Well, that seemed to go alright, for now at least. What d'you think, Edward? Will she be okay?'

Edward came and sat beside Lucy and put his arm around her shoulders. 'You did brilliantly, just right. And like most children, Daisy took it at face value. I'm sure she'll have questions but in her own time; she'll ask when she's ready. She seems more concerned for you, she's such a poppet. And that's thanks to you Lucy. You're such a great mum.'

Lucy relaxed into Edward. 'Thanks, I do my best! And having Daisy helps me to keep things in perspective. I can't just fall apart, can I? That wouldn't do anyone any good. I still can't believe what's happened today, though. I always struggled to work Mum out, to understand what made her tick; I suppose this explains it. And in her head, maybe the reason she didn't tell me about not being my mum was to spare me from more turmoil growing up; it just meant she kept it all inside which drove her, well, a bit crazy. How incredibly sad; what a wasted life.'

'But it wasn't a wasted life. She loved you and Daisy completely, even though she couldn't always show it. Who knows what would have happened to you, and her, if she hadn't brought you up?'

'Maybe you're right. And now I need to find out my story, see if there are any of those 'others' out there that Mum alluded to in her letter. Wish me luck Edward, I think I'm going to need it.'

Chapter 8

1982

'Hi honey, I'm home!' Will called in a fake American accent, as he came through the front door.

'Dadeee!' he heard, as the kitchen door burst open and Michael came hurtling along the hall and into his arms. 'Hello little fella,' he said, as he lifted Michael up, swung him round and planted a kiss on his head. 'Have you had a good day. Where's Mummy?'

'In here,' Rachel called from the kitchen. 'And no, we haven't had a good day. We got soaked when we went to toddler group, Mikey had a tantrum when it was time to leave – I swear he's reached the terrible twos already – and Matty's teething so he's been grizzling all day. His gums are so red. Yogurt is the only thing I can get him to eat.' Matty was sitting in his highchair with yogurt all around his mouth, while Michael clung on to Will's leg squealing, 'Up! Up!'

'Thank God you're home. You can take over now,' continued Rachel over Michael's screeches, and took a swig from a glass of wine.

'Bit early to be on the booze, isn't it?' said Will, as he lifted Michael up again and went to the sink for a cloth to clean Matty's mouth.

'Oh don't start!' replied Rachel. 'It's been a bugger of a day and there was half a bottle left in the fridge, so I thought, why not? I'm off for a bath.' Rachel picked up the glass and the bottle and headed upstairs.

'Leave the water when you've finished and I'll bath the boys,' called Will after her. He gave a heavy sigh, took them into the sitting room and turned on the television. The floor was strewn with discarded toys. Matty crawled into the midst of them and started chewing on a stacking ring. Michael grabbed a book and climbed onto Will's knee. As Will distractedly turned the pages, while Michael made as if to read the book in toddler gobbledegook, he worried about Rachel. This wasn't the first time he'd come home to find a half-finished bottle of wine on the table, or an empty one in the bin. Fine if she wanted to get sozzled on nights out, but hitting the bottle in the middle of the day with the babies to look after was another matter. He dreaded it, but knew he'd have to have that conversation with her.

***

Later, when Will had bathed the boys and settled them in bed, while Rachel tidied up the living room and cooked a spaghetti bolognaise for supper, he broached the subject again. It didn't go well.

'Rach, something's niggling me and I've got to say it. I'm worried about your drinking in the day when you've got the boys to look after.' He could almost see her hackles rising.

'For God's sake Will, it was only because I'd had a crap day and there was some left in the fridge. It's not as if I do it every day.'

'No, but it's not the first time, is it? I've seen the empty bottles in the bin Rach.' He tried to say it gently, but it fell on deaf ears. Rachel stormed out of the kitchen. When Will had cleared up the supper dishes, he found her slumped on the sofa in the living room. He tentatively sat down beside her. 'Look Rach, I know you like a drink, as do I, but my concern is the boys. I mean, is it because you're struggling to cope? Is there anything I can do to help? It can be a slippery slope you know.'

'Don't patronise me Will, of course I can cope and no, I don't need any help. You sound just like my parents.'

'Oh, so they've noticed as well, have they?'

Rachel groaned and Will was waiting for her to storm off again. But instead, looking rather sheepish, she opened up. 'Look Will. I do have a bit of history with drink, but it's not serious. Me and a friend started drinking at her house when we were at school, about twelve I suppose. Her dad owned an off licence and there was always booze in the house, so we'd help ourselves. When I was sixteen, I was supposedly at a party at her house, but instead we went out with a group of older hippy friends. I got so drunk I ended up in hospital having my stomach pumped. Apparently, I nearly choked on my own vomit. Mum and Dad made me swear I'd never get in that state again. They threatened to ground me for six months, so I just sort of took off for a few days with the same group. It was that really hot summer of 1976 – d'you remember it? – so we just sat in the park all day drinking and found places to sleep each night under the stars. Of course, the police got involved and I got hell because I was underage. I was quite the celebrity at school when I went back!'

'Bloody hell Rach –' Will was about to say more when the phone rang. 'Hello? Oh, hi Mum. Mum? Are you in a call box? Is everything okay?' Will could hear his mother, but she sounded odd and there was a sob in her voice.

'Oh Will. It's dad, he's had a heart attack. He's in hospital and it's serious. Can you come down?'

'Oh no. Mum, are you okay? When? Where are Dan and the twins?'

'We're all here at the hospital. Treliske. I haven't got long before my money runs out. If you can get down, please come.'

'I will, of course I will. I'll make arrangements and come straight away. Oh Mum. Send my love to Dad and tell him I'll be there soon.'

***

Two hours later Will was on the road to Cornwall. Frantic phone calls had been made to his boss (to sanction compassionate leave) and to Rachel's parents (to ask them to keep a subtle eye on Rach), while she threw some clothes into a case for Will. He kissed the sleeping boys goodbye and was on the road. The conversation about Rachel's drinking past and current habit was forgotten, at least for now.

Will arrived at the Royal Cornwall Hospital at six in the morning, having driven through the night, with only a couple of stops for coffee from a flask and a pee behind a bush. Why was Cornwall such a long way? Not for the first time, Will wondered if his move to London had been a mistake. They hadn't been back to Porthleven for over three months, not since before Matty was born, and their last annual trip in July had been hard work, with Michael just toddling (Pippa had moved ornaments and breakables out of reach) and Rachel heavily pregnant. Thinking back, Will realised that all the trips to Cornwall with Rachel had been difficult (on his insistence, they had spent a week there each summer); there was a mutual wariness between Rachel and his parents, and it was a continuing source of disappointment to him that she didn't feel the love for the county that was as much a part of him as if it were another limb.

He was directed to the intensive care ward but was unable to see his father straight away. He found Uncle Jethro, Seth's brother, slumped in a chair in the corridor. 'Uncle Jethro,' said Will, 'what's happened? Where's Mum?'

'Ah Will, glad you're here Bud,' said Jethro, as he heaved himself out of the chair, and the two men embraced in a bear hug. 'Your mum and the others have gone to get some sleep; they were here 'til after midnight. I'm keeping vigil till they come back in the mornin'.' Immediately, Will felt comforted by Jethro's soft Cornish accent and mild manner. 'Seth collapsed at work yesterday and was rushed straight here. Heart attack, so they say. Talking of a heart bypass, open heart surgery, all sorts. They reckon he'll pull through, he's out of danger now, so that's the main thing.'

Will could feel the tears welling and he sat down heavily on one of the hard plastic chairs. Jethro sat beside him and put an arm round his shoulder. 'It's alright Buddy. It'll be alright.'

'Oh God, what a mess,' said Will, and knew he wasn't only thinking of his father's plight. 'When will they let me see him?' He walked over to the ward just as a nurse was coming through the door. 'I'm Will Carne, he's my dad and I've just driven from London, can I see him, please?' he pleaded. The nurse took pity on him and said he could see Seth for a few minutes but not to disturb him while he's sleeping. Will went and sat by his father's bedside, alarmed by the array of wires and tubes protruding from him, and the bags of unidentifiable liquids hanging in bags on hooks around him. 'Oh God,' he whispered, 'please don't let Dad die.'

Suddenly Seth's eyelids fluttered. 'Will, is that you?' he said weakly. 'You came.'

''Course I came, Dad. They've only let me in for a minute and I'm not supposed to disturb you so take it easy. How're you doing?'

'Been better Will, been better,' and with that Seth's eyes closed again, but he had the faintest of smiles on his lips.

***

The next few days were a blur of hospital visits, rushed meals, meetings with doctors and consultants and sleepless nights. In the end, Seth hadn't needed further surgery, after a successful angioplasty, and it seemed he wouldn't need a bypass, but it was all a bit technical for the family and they were just relieved he was on the road to recovery.

They took it in turns to visit and Will was just off to see Seth, when Tamsin arrived at the house. They almost collided on the front doorstep. 'Will!' said Tamsin. 'Tam!' said Will, simultaneously. They looked at one another for a second and fell into an embrace. 'I'm so sorry, Will. I heard about Seth. How is he?' said Tam, as they pulled apart.

'He's going to be okay, but it's been bloody awful to be honest. Poor Mum, she's on her knees. I'm just off to the hospital now. We're taking it in turns.'

'I won't hold you up. Is there anything I can do?'

'Sweet of you to ask but I can't think of anything. It's all a bit of a muddle right now, but Mum might be glad of some help when I've gone. I know she's got Dan and the twins but when they're back at work and college, she might need a bit of support. Especially when Dad comes home.'

'Don't worry, I'll rally the troops and I'll get Dad to send over some bread and pasties to keep your lot fed.' Tamsin's family owned the bakery in Porthleven and produced some of the finest pasties in the county. 'How long are you staying? Are the family with you?' Tamsin asked, as she looked enquiringly past Will towards the house.

'No, I came as soon as I heard. I'll probably stay till the weekend, then I'll have to get back.' Will's heart felt heavy, and his head conflicted, as he thought of returning to London. He was desperate to see the boys but was confused about his feelings towards Rachel. 'Look, shall we have a drink later, if you can make it? I'll be back from the hospital about seven. Shall we go to the Ship? Have a proper catch up before I go?'

'I'd love that, if it's not dragging you away from the others when they need you?' Tam's eyes were dancing as she looked up at Will, who was a good six inches taller than her.

'Mum's going to see Dad this evening then staying with a friend in Truro, so she doesn't have to drive back. She wants to be there again in the morning to see the consultant. They're talking of discharging him in a few days. The others will just be flopping in front of the telly I expect, so they won't miss me. Look, I'd better be off, or I'll miss afternoon visiting, - they're very strict! See you later then?'

'Seven at The Ship it is!' Will leant to kiss Tam on the cheek at the same time as she went to kiss him and inadvertently their lips met. They jumped back as if hit by an electric shock, stared at one another for a moment, then laughed and went in for a hug instead. Tam walked off down the drive with a spring in her step as Will went to his car. Suddenly, his heart felt lighter than it had for weeks.

***

Will felt a mix of excitement and nostalgia as he walked along the harbour to The Ship Inn. It was as familiar and comforting as an old friend, the building standing sentinel over the harbour since the 17th century. It was a rough, autumnal night, the sea high and the waves pounding the rocks and breakwater, but a roaring fire welcomed him in the pub.

'Alright Will? Long time no see. Usual, is it?' said the barman. 'How's your old man?'

'Hi Josh. You haven't forgotten then? Dad's doing okay, out of danger now and hopefully coming home soon.'

'Here you are Bud,' he said, as he placed a pint of Will's usual tipple on the bar. 'Glad Seth's doing alright. Tam's over there, she's got her drink.' He nodded to where Tam was sitting in the window.

'I've missed this place,' said Will as he joined her. 'No pubs like this in London. No one knows who you are, let alone what you drink.' He gave a heavy sigh. 'And I miss the sea so much.'

'So how's it going in London? How are your lovely little boys? It seems like you've been gone forever,' replied Tam. 'Do you think you'll ever move back here like you planned, you know, make your fortune then buy a fishing boat and join the Carne fleet?'

'Oh Tam, I don't know. The longer I'm away, the more I miss the place, and the people,' he said, as he looked intently into Tam's lovely eyes. 'But my life's in London now, with the boys and Rachel. She'll never want to leave; she's born and bred there. My Cornish dream seems further away than ever.' He hoped he wasn't sounding bitter.

'But you must be happy, with a great job in the bank, with Rachel and a family? I bet you're a terrific dad.' Tam was so open, so straightforward, so kind, that Will found himself telling her about the unplanned arrivals of Michael and Matty and of Rachel's drinking. 'It's all happened so fast. After our first visit to Cornwall, remember? When Rach disgraced herself at the barbeque, I went back thinking I might end it with her but then she got pregnant with Mikey and here we are. Oh God, Tam, why did I leave Cornwall?'

Tam leant across the table and laid her hand on Will's. 'I'm so sorry, I had no idea. I assumed you were flying high in London, that life here was becoming just a childhood memory. Oh Will, why *did* you go?' They held hands across the table, neither speaking, lost in their memories of a shared history. They'd known each other since they were toddlers, growing up together in the close-knit community of Porthleven, with the beaches and sea as their playground. Like Will, many of their friends had either left the village to work elsewhere or for higher education. But Tam had stayed; she had no wish to leave her beloved home. She'd taken an apprenticeship as a jeweller and was now starting out on her own. Her exquisite pieces sold well at craft fairs and from a shop in St Ives. Her dream was to open her own gallery in Porthleven. She and Will always had a special bond in their group, and now Will admitted to himself that he wished it had been more. But it was too late to hope for that now, his life was on a different tack altogether. 'I'm sorry, Tam,' he thought.

'Sorry about what?' Tam replied, and Will realised he'd spoken his thoughts out loud.

'What? Oh, sorry, just thinking aloud.'

'About what?' Tam had an amused look and raised her eyebrows playfully.

'Bloody hell, Tam. You can read me like a book. Always could. You know I love you, don't you?' He felt a rush of relief at uttering the words he had wanted to say for so long and started laughing at the ridiculousness of the situation.

'Yep, I think I do. And I'll always love you Will. And a fat lot of good that will do us now!' She was laughing too.

'God, what a mess! What are we supposed to do?'

'Nothing, I guess. We've never done anything before and, just as long as we never lose our friendship ….' her words petered out and suddenly they weren't laughing any more. 'Let's change the subject Will, this is too difficult. Did I tell you I've made a new range of jewellery, silver, based on a starfish design. Here, I've got some photos.' They pored over pictures of Tam's new range until a few more of their friends turned up and their 'moment' was gone.

***

When Will arrived back at his parents' house, feeling more conflicted than ever, the twins were in bed, but Dan was still up playing his guitar. 'Any news of Dad?' asked Will.

'No. Mum's going to ring when they've seen the consultant tomorrow. Oh, Rachel rang earlier, just to see how things are. I said you were at the pub with Tam. She said don't bother to ring back.' Will's heart sank like a stone.

Chapter 9

2016

Lucy woke with a racing heart, her mind buzzing with thoughts of the day ahead: Jake was coming with the key to unlock the fateful safe; how would that work with Emily here; how would Daisy be after yesterday's bombshell and what was she going to give the girls for lunch? She hauled herself out of bed and stood under a steaming shower, then turned the water to cold for a few seconds, to clear her head. When she returned to her bedroom, Daisy was on the bed and bounced across it on her knees for a cuddle. 'Mum, can we light the fire pit today and toast marshmallows when Emily's here?'

The last thing Lucy felt like doing was slaving over a hot fire pit, but maybe Jake would help. 'That's a good idea. I'll have to check we've got some.'

'We have. I brought a bag of them back from Brownies when they didn't get used at the campfire, remember? So many people brought them, they had loads left over.'

'You're right, as always,' laughed Lucy. At least that solved part of the lunch problem. 'Come on, go and get dressed and we can have some breakfast. Emily will be here at ten.'

Lucy was distracted during breakfast; her thoughts returning to the safe and the secrets it would reveal. She was, in equal measure, desperate to open it and terrified of delving into an unknown past.

'Here they are, Mum. Two bags. That should be enough.' Daisy had been rummaging in a cupboard and unearthed the marshmallows.

'I should think it would! I doubt you'll need them all, there's only two of you! By the way, Jake is coming today. He's visiting his parents in Tunbridge Wells and wants to drop by. I'm going to ask him to help me with a few more of Granny's things while he's here.'

'Don't you mean Great Granny? Anyway, he can roast some marshmallows too, then we *will* need both bags.' Daisy plonked them on the worktop and skipped off before being called back by Lucy to help clear the table. Obviously, yesterday's revelation hasn't caused undue concern yet, thought Lucy. Thank goodness for Emily's visit, which seems far more important.

Emily arrived on time and the girls immediately went to play in the Wendy house. It was a wonderful wooden play-house, built by George shortly after they'd moved to Kent, with two floors and a proper staircase. It stood at the far end of the large garden, almost hidden by a tall bamboo, but just visible enough for Lucy to keep an eye on it from the kitchen window. George and Suzannah had bought their house in Tunbridge Wells in the boom years of the late seventies. It was a shrewd move given the recession and financial crash that were to follow. George had a successful building firm in London and invested in the large red brick house in a smart residential area of the town, not far from the high point of Mount Ephraim and the Common on which stood the incongruous, yet iconic, Wellington Rocks. It was an imposing residence with tall pseudo-Elizabethan chimneys, leaded light windows and a solid oak front door dressed with chunky wrought iron fittings. The house and garden, surrounded by mature trees and shrubs, were set well back from the road and reached by a long, gated, drive. Sometime in the early eighties – Lucy didn't know exactly when – they had moved from London to live there permanently and, although she enjoyed her garden when well, Lucy couldn't understand why her mother was so unhappy in what was, undeniably, a dream home. As a child, Lucy had spent hours in the Wendy house, where she played at make believe and escaped the oppressive presence of her mother/grandmother. Now, it was a joy to see Daisy playing in it – even at the grand old age of ten – as she had done ever since she was able to toddle down the garden.

Lucy followed the girls into the garden and gave the fire pit a once over – it hadn't been used for many months – and collected some logs from the wood store, ready for lighting it later. Her phone pinged with a text from Jake.

> On my way over. Let me know if you need me to pick anything up. Jx

All good, see you soon. Lx, she replied. There was plenty of food left over from the posh lunch yesterday and the girls would be happy with sandwiches and crisps in the Wendy house.

***

An hour later Lucy and Jake were sitting on the floor in front of the open wardrobe doors in Susannah's bedroom, coffee mugs in hand. 'Well, are you ready?' said Jake, as he drained the last of his coffee and held out the safe key to Lucy.

'Ready as I'll ever be, I guess.' She took the key in her trembling hand, leant into the wardrobe and unlocked the safe. 'Here goes,' she said, as she opened the little steel door. She felt inside and pulled out two bundles held together with elastic bands. The first was a stack of photos, the second a wad of official looking papers.

'Why don't you start with the photos,' said Jake gently. 'The papers might take more brainpower.'

Lucy gave a weak laugh but didn't feel like making lack of brainpower jokes. She carefully removed the elastic band from around the photos and laid them out on the floor. There was a mixture of colour photos, faded with a seventies sepia tinge, and black and white. She looked helplessly at Jake. 'Where do I start?' she pleaded, then immediately picked up one of the black and white pictures and turned it over. '*Rachel 1960*', she read from the caption scrawled on the back in a fine script. She turned it over to study the tiny baby lying in an old-fashioned carrycot, then passed it to Jake. 'Who the hell is Rachel? My mother?' she said bitterly. She felt numb as she picked up the next, more formal, photo. It was an official school photo and on the back was written '*Rachel 1972*'. Another followed; this time it was Rachel in 1978, in her final term at secondary school, according to the caption. She passed them to Jake, hardly seeing the girl smiling out at her from those moments frozen in time. 'Are you alright Lucy?' he asked. He laid his hand on her arm. 'You can stop if you want, you don't have to do it all in one go.'

'I'm just so *angry*. How could this have happened? *What* the hell happened? Is this all I'm going to get, a pile of fading images with names and faces that mean nothing to me? How am I supposed to work it all out from this lot? Right now, I hate my mother, or grandmother or whatever the hell she was.' Lucy burst into tears. Jake took her in his arms and let her cry. He didn't try and tell her it would be alright, that she didn't really hate her mother/grandmother, he just held her until the sobs subsided.

'Mum, can we have a drink and a biscuit?' came a shout up the stairs from Daisy.

'Oh God, the girls,' groaned Lucy.

'You stay here, I'll sort them out with drinks.' Jake went bounding downstairs while Lucy tried to pull herself together. She ran a flannel under the cold tap in Susannah's en-suite and dabbed at her face. By the time Jake returned she felt slightly better and had started going through the colour photos.

'All sorted,' said Jake, as he sat beside Lucy on the bed. 'I told Daisy you were just finishing up and would be down soon. They've taken their drinks into the garden and are deep into some game on their screens. Hope that's okay?'

'Thanks Jake. We'll get them off the screens at lunchtime and light the fire pit afterwards.' Lucy flicked the photos over and read out the captions on each one.

'*Rachel and Becky 1979 – Barclays Bank*', '*Rachel and the boys 1982*', '*Rachel and Becky 1985 – Eastbourne*'. Well, a fat lot of use those are, how are they going to help me find out my past?' She turned them back over to study the faces, but another shout came up the stairs.

'Muuum, what are you doing? We want to light the fire pit.'

'This is hopeless,' said Lucy. 'I can't concentrate on this while the girls are downstairs. Let's leave it for now. I can always have another go when Daisy's in bed tonight.'

'If that's what you want Lucy. Come on then, let's get this fire pit going.'

In the end, it was the best thing they could've done. It was a perfect summer's day, deliciously warm but not stifling, and they ate lunch in the garden, Lucy and Jake savouring the leftovers of the *Fortnum's* picnic hamper. Jake did a cracking job of lighting the fire pit and even made some toasting prongs out of bamboo, when it was obvious they weren't going to unearth the metal ones discarded in the depths of the shed at the end of last summer. 'Wow, those are cool,' said Daisy.

'I wasn't a Boy Scout for nothing, you know,' replied Jake with a grin.

'Me and Ems are in the Brownies, aren't we Em? But we go up to Guides next term. The marshmallows were left over from our campfire at the end of term.'

'We ate so many that one of our friends, Alice, was sick all over the place. Wasn't she Daisy?' chimed in Emily.

'It was disgusting! But it hasn't put me off them.' And with that, everyone held their bamboo sticks over the fire and watched as the marshmallows turned brown and gooey. Lucy was able to push the contents of the safe to the back of her mind and realised she was having fun. They played a mad game of hide-and-seek, 'to run off all that sugar,' said Jake, and then giant Jenga on the patio.

Later in the afternoon, Chloe arrived to collect Emily, at which point the girls decided they *must* have another game in the Wendy house and ran off. 'Time for a cup of tea before you go Chloe?' asked Jake.

'I'd love one, I'm gasping. Sainsburys was manic. I hate food shopping!' Chloe and Lucy sat on the patio as Jake went off to organise some tea.

'Thanks for having Emily, Lucy. Are you sure it's not too much, you've got so much on and to be honest, you look exhausted.'

'I am rather …' Lucy's voice trembled, and, through blurred teary eyes, Lucy explained about the revelations of the last twenty-four hours. '… so now I've got all these photos and a pile of papers, and I've got to play detective to find out my true past. It's like some sick riddle mum's left me from beyond the grave.'

'Oh Lucy, I'm sorry. As if you didn't have enough to cope with already.' Chloe took Lucy's hand. 'Look, you can't possibly deal with this on your own. Why don't we have Daisy to sleep over tonight and tomorrow so you can have some time to process it, without having to worry about her. Will Jake be able to support you? We haven't got anything planned so it will do us a favour to have Emily occupied. If Daisy gets upset about her granny/great granny, we can always run her home.'

Lucy was amazed at the relief she felt. 'Oh would you? Chloe, you're a life saver. I'm in bits to be honest,' and, with that, the tears came again. 'Sorry, it's just …..'

'Hey, it's okay.' Chloe got up to give Lucy a hug as Jake appeared with the tea.

***

Daisy went off happily with Emily and Chloe after throwing a few clothes, and Little Bear, into her rucksack. Jake and Lucy cleared up the paraphernalia of the day spent in the garden and flopped down on the sofa with glasses of chilled white wine. 'I don't know how you do it. It's exhausting looking after ten-year-olds!' said Jake.

'Yep,' replied Lucy. 'Especially right now with everything going on. It's so good of Chloe to have Daisy again. I feel a bit guilty really.'

'Hey, come on. She wouldn't have offered if she didn't want to. Now, what do you want to do next? How about we put the photos and papers out on the dining room table and go through them properly?'

'Yes okay.' Lucy felt the weight of despair like a millstone round her neck, but knew she had to continue the crazy journey her mother had set her on. It *has* to get easier, she thought, as Jake took her hands and heaved her out of the soft sofa cushions.

'Come here lovely girl.' He pulled her into a hug. 'You'll get through this you know. You may not feel like it now, but you will. And I'll be here to help.' He gave her a soft kiss before pulling away. 'Come on, no distractions, let's do this.' Jake winked at Lucy and headed up the stairs. Ten minutes later, the photos and papers were arranged in some sort of order across the dining table.

They sat together and studied the photos again, this time more thoroughly. 'I think we have to assume that Rachel is my mother, and the black and white shots are of her as a baby and through her school years. Agree?' Lucy suddenly felt very business-like, like a detective with a new case. She almost wanted a white board on which to pin the photos. She felt no emotional connection at all to the woman looking out from the pictures.

'Agree.'

'Do we assume Becky is a friend of Rachel's? Or maybe a sister? No, that doesn't make sense and they look nothing alike. I don't get why she's included in the pack but there must be some significance. Do you think there's any resemblance between Rachel and me?'

'You've got the same hair – lustrous waves, but hers is a sort of auburn colour; her eyes look blue. Maybe she and Becky worked together in the bank? In Eastbourne perhaps?'

'Then there are these of Rachel and 'the boys'. Are they her boys? I was born in 1984 so, if Rachel is my mother, did she have other children before me? My life, Jake, maybe I've got long lost brothers somewhere? And if so, what happened to them? Perhaps they are Becky's and Rachel is their godmother or something?'

Jake studied the latest photo of Rachel and Becky in 1985. 'She doesn't look as well in this last photo. She's very thin and her hair looks lank.'

'Mmm, bad hair day perhaps.' She picked up a badly creased photo that looked as if it had been screwed up at some point and flattened out again. '*Will 1981*' was written on the back. 'Oh!'

'What?'

'I don't know, I just felt a sort of jolt inside. Does he look familiar? I'm not sure, there is *something* though.' She passed it to Jake.

'So, who is he? Rachel's husband? Becky's husband?' They looked through the photos again.

'If he's Rachel's husband, that makes him my father! Oh good grief, this isn't getting us very far, is it? We'd make rubbish detectives!' said Lucy after a while.

'Shall we move on to the papers, see if they shine any light? Let's top up our glasses first; are we allowed to drink on duty?'

'Definitely!'

Jake headed off to the kitchen and returned a few minutes later with the wine bottle and some nibbles. 'Thought we might need some sustenance.'

'Good idea,' said Lucy distractedly. 'These papers are birth certificates, and then there's these few letters. Let's start with the certificates.' Lucy spread them out on the table. 'So, Rachel was born in 1960 to Susannah and George Askwith. So she *must be* my mother. Unless there was another daughter.' Lucy returned to the photo of Rachel taken at the end of her school career, and really studied it. 'I think I've got her nose, look.'

'No, yours is definitely cuter, but maybe there is a likeness.' Lucy managed a weak smile.

'So, what next? Oh, this is my birth certificate. I didn't know she had it. I've only ever had a short version; Susannah said the full form got lost when we moved here. She was priceless, wasn't she? The short version doesn't have the parents' names, so I never knew she and George weren't mine.' She examined the certificate. 'Hang on, this states Rachel Askwith as my mother, but the father is blank.

Why would that be? Don't you have to include the father's name? Perhaps she didn't know who he was.'

'I think the mother can decide whether or not to include the father's name.'

'Oh yes, you're right. I remember now being asked if I wanted Danny's name on Daisy's birth certificate. I didn't see any reason not to, but obviously Rachel did.'

Jake picked up the last certificate in the pile. 'This is Susannah's. Born in 1942 in London, to Albert and Lilly Goodman. It says Albert was a Sand & Gravel Merchant. So, these are your grandparents, no, hang on, your great grandparents. Sorry, I still get confused.'

'Me too, it does my head in to be honest. I never knew them, but Susannah didn't talk about them, or George's parents. I just assumed they were dead, but I suppose they could still be alive. Who knows?'

Jake noticed that Lucy had started referring to her grandmother/mother as Susannah. Was this to save confusion or was she distancing herself from the woman who had lived a lie.

'What's the time Jake? We've been at this for hours,' and then Lucy's phone rang.

'Hi Lucy, it's Mark.' It took Lucy a moment to drag herself back into the present. 'It's Ellie, she's had the baby, a little girl. Two weeks early, and completely took us by surprise, but all is well.'

'Oh Mark, that's great news! A girl, how sweet. When? How big? Have you got a name?'

Mark was laughing. 'In the early hours of this morning. 3.4kg. And we're calling her Lyra Jane. The Jane is after my mum.'

'I love that. Congrats to you both. When can we come and visit?'

'Maybe tomorrow, or the day after? Why don't you ring tomorrow and see how Ellie's doing. She's asleep now and I'm just ringing round everyone.'

'Good idea. Jake from school is here, so we'll raise a glass and I'll see you very soon.'

'Thanks Lucy. And how are you doing?' The concern in Mark's voice nearly set her off again. Her sudden excitement at some good news died and she felt deflated again in a moment, but she didn't want to rain on Mark and Ellie's parade. 'I'm fine Mark. Send our love to Ellie, bye now,' she said, as brightly as she could.

'I take it Ellie's had her baby then?' said Jake, as Lucy ended the call. 'Did I hear we're going to wet the baby's head? Sounds like a great plan. Look, why don't we call it a night and deal with the letters tomorrow. You must be completely wrung out.'

After some reticence, Lucy agreed. At first, she thought she wouldn't sleep if she left the letters unopened, but Jake took charge and led her into the sitting room, closing the door on the emerging story of Lucy's past. 'Let's watch some mindless telly, it'll give our brains a rest. Don't know about you, but mine's hurting.' He found an old episode of *Faulty Towers* and left Lucy reclining on the sofa while he went to the kitchen. He found a bottle of Prosecco which he put in the freezer to cool quickly, while he rustled up scrambled eggs, with the last of the smoked salmon from *Fortnum and Mason*. When he returned to the sitting room, he was glad to see Lucy laughing at John Cleese giving his Austin 1100 a 'damn good thrashing' with the branch of a tree. After eating supper on their knees and toasting the arrival of Lyra Jane, they snuggled up together and, in a moment, were asleep.

Chapter 10
1982

Will arrived in London after a tedious drive back from Cornwall. He'd wanted to walk on the beach at Loe Bar, to visit his thin place before leaving, but it was drizzling, and he didn't want to sit in wet clothes all the way back. Seth had been discharged from hospital and the wider family rallied round to provide support, so Will felt he needn't stay longer, although it was more of a wrench than ever to leave.

Michael and Matty were already in bed by the time he arrived, and he crept into their rooms to give them a kiss goodnight. His heart melted at the sight of the sleeping boys. Please Dad, get well, he thought. I want you to get to know these little chaps and you haven't even met Matty yet. Don't let it be too late.

Rachel was looking gorgeous, hair and make-up done to perfection, and a far cry from the frazzled mum he'd left behind a few days before. 'I've missed you so much, Will.' She pressed into him and kissed him sensuously. 'So have the boys. They've been asking about you all the time. Mum's been great, though. She came round most days and Becky called in too. How was your dad? Is he going to be alright? Was it awful? Such a long way to go and was it a terrible drive back in this weather? Sit down and I'll get you something to eat.'

'Hang on, Rach. Can we just slow down a minute?' He flet slightly alarmed by her Tigger-like manner, as if she was on some sort of adrenaline rush.

'Yes, sorry. I'm just so pleased to see you. Have you noticed how clean and tidy the house is? Mum and I gave it a good going over while you were away.'

What was this? Some attempt to placate Will after their spat before he went away. Was she trying to compensate? 'It's great.' He didn't know what else to say; his head (and his heart?) was still very much in Cornwall.

Rachel snuggled up to Will on the sofa, kissing him gently. At first, he felt guilty at enjoying the sensations that were stirring, his thoughts flipping back to the turmoil of the last few days, but then his body responded and soon he and Rachel were making love, Will driven by a primal need for satisfaction and comfort in his confusion.

***

Back at work, Will's boss and colleagues were sympathetic but the business of the bank was as demanding as ever. With unemployment at its highest for fifty years, staggeringly high interest rates, and a recession triggered by a tight monetary policy introduced to fight rising inflation, financial stability was a thing of the past. Work life was pressured. Is this what had caused Dad's heart attack? he thought. Although the pressures in a provincial branch in Cornwall were unlikely to be as marked as those in the city, Seth was a branch manager in turbulent times.

'Hi Will. Good to see you back. How's your dad?' Becky came into the small office kitchen with her coffee cup.

'He's on the road to recovery I think, Becky. He's been discharged from hospital which I guess is a good thing. Thanks for popping in to see Rach while I was away.' He wanted to say more but didn't know whether he should confide in Becky, but she placed her hand on his arm. 'Actually Will, can you get away at lunch time? I think we need to talk about Rachel.'

Will's heart sank. 'Yes of course, I was rather wanting a chat. I'll meet you in the banking hall at half twelve.'

By twelve forty-five, Will and Becky were tucked into a booth at the café, with steaming cups of tea. While Will was wondering how to start the conversation about Rachel, Becky launched in. 'I'm sorry to add to your problems Will, but I'm really worried about Rach. I went round to see her because Anna had asked if I would. Anna told me that you'd asked her to keep a surreptitious eye on Rach while you were away, because of the drinking, but she'd seen no evidence of it. But she thought Rach would be careful to cover up when she was around, so asked if I would turn up unannounced. It felt pretty sneaky to be honest, but when I arrived, she was halfway down a bottle of wine. The boys were tucked up in bed because I asked if I could have a peep at them – they are *so* gorgeous – and I don't know how long she'd been drinking. She was so pleased to see me – I think she'd had a tough day with the boys – and persuaded me to stay for a drink. When I went to get a glass from the kitchen, I had a look in the bin. There were two more bottles there.'

'Oh grief! I thought after our row before I went, she would stop. Do you think she's got a problem? Apparently, she started drinking when she was quite young, and by that I mean she wasn't even a teenager.'

'Yes, she's told me about that, almost like she was proud of the reputation it gave her at school. I don't know Will. I didn't say anything to her when I was there, I didn't want to risk our friendship and wanted to talk to you first. D'you think she's finding it hard to cope with the boys or could it be post-natal depression?'

'I don't know. She's not easy to talk to. If I mention anything about the drinking, she takes it as a personal criticism and goes off the deep end. You know how feisty she can be!'

'I do indeed, she's certainly strong willed. Well look, you know I'm always happy to help; Si and me both are, but I also wanted to tell you that we're going to be moving out of town. Si's got a job in Eastbourne, and we hope to move in the next few months. We want to start a family and don't want to bring our kids up in London. Oh, sorry, that's not to say ….'

'It's okay. I get it. I just wish we'd done things the right way round. I'd love to bring Michael and Matty up in Cornwall.' Although Will wondered if he'd even be with Rachel if she hadn't become pregnant.

***

After Will's chat with Becky, he found himself watching Rachel like a hawk, for signs of drinking during the day, but her enthusiasm that had greeted him on his return from Cornwall continued, and for a few weeks, all was calm. He even started seeing the fun-loving Rachel he'd first met. At the weekends, they took the children for Autumn walks in the park, kicking up fallen leaves and feeding the ducks with stale bread. They delighted in watching Michael enjoy his favourite pastime – chasing pigeons across the grass and squealing with delight as they took off as one into the blue sky, while Matty writhed in his pushchair, desperate to get out and join in the fun. At times like these, Will could almost convince himself that he was happy in London.

Rachel became a leading light in the toddler group and volunteered to arrange the forthcoming Christmas party. She threw herself into the task, in typical Rachel style, and found she had a flair for organising other members of the playgroup committee and soon had them signing up for baking, making decorations and co-ordinating games. The kitchen table was covered with lists and spreadsheets, and Will was just happy that it wasn't covered in empty wine bottles.

Will knew he must make another trip to Cornwall to see Seth, and suggested to Rachel that they go for a weekend before Christmas.

'Look Will, why don't you go on your own. I've got so much on here, with the party to plan and all the other pre-Christmas stuff. And I've got the girls' night out on Saturday.'

Will's heart sank. How would that go, he wondered. She hadn't been drinking lately, as far as he knew, but would a night out with the girls be another stumbling block? He must remember to ask Becky to look out for her.

'I tell you what, why don't you take Mikey with you? Your mum and dad would love to see him, and he'd think it was great to get some dad time. And it will be easier if I've only got Matty to cope with.'

Anything to make Rach's life easier, thought Will. 'Okay, but we must all go down soon. They haven't met Matty yet.'

Rachel snuggled into Will. 'I know. We'll go down sometime in the New Year. We could've had them here for Christmas but with your dad still recovering they're not likely to want to make the journey, are they?'

'No and I wouldn't be happy with them doing it either. Alright, Mikey and I will go. We'll drive down overnight on Friday, and I'll take Monday off work and come back then.'

'Good idea. Come on then, bedtime. If you won't be here at the weekend, let's make the most of tonight!'

***

As Will crossed the Tamar Bridge into Cornwall, the sun was rising. The late November days were short, but this morning's sunrise was spectacular and promised a fine walk on the beach later. His heart soared at the thought. As he drove further into Cornwall, the landscape became more and more familiar until he was driving the last few miles towards Helston and on to Porthleven.

Pippa enveloped him in a hug as soon as he was out of the car. 'Will, it's so good to see you. Thanks for coming down again.' She leant into the back to lift a sleeping Michael out of his car seat. He awoke at the disturbance and Will wondered if he would be grumpy, but he frowned for a moment at his grandmother, then stuck his thumb in his mouth and snuggled into her shoulder. 'Hello Mikey,' she said softly. 'It's lovely to see you. What a long car journey you've had. Would you like something to eat?' Mikey nodded but kept his thumb firmly in his mouth.

'How's Dad doing?' asked Will, as he carried their paraphernalia into the house. Always so much to bring with a toddler. 'Oh, hi Dad, how's it going?' Seth was waiting for them in the hall. Will dropped the bags and folded him into a hug. 'You had us worried back then.' His eyes moistened as he held his father close.

'It'll take more than a heart attack to get rid of me! Come on through to the kitchen. Mum's planning a full English for you. Hello Mikey.' Seth gently ruffled his hair as Pippa carried him through to the warm kitchen.

Half an hour later, Will was completely cocooned in the heart of his family. Evie and Grace had welcomed him with big sisterly hugs before moving quickly on to Mikey, who, in their opinion, was far cuter and worth way more of their attention. Dan had emerged from his bedroom, his hair still mussed from sleep, and given Will a brotherly slap on the back. 'Alright Bud?'

'Yeah, you?' Will replied. Few words passed between them, but the brothers were close and not many were needed.

***

Over the weekend, Will's fears for Seth's health receded as he saw for himself that he was making a good recovery. He was thankful for this time to be with the family and to see how they were sticking close together, as if Seth's heart attack had forged a closer bond between them. He longed to be part of this close-knit unit with his own family but knew this would never happen, that Rachel would not be persuaded to move to Cornwall.

'Penny for them,' said Pippa. They were standing on the beach at Loe Bar, watching the mighty waves break on the shore, listening to the hiss of the shingle as it was sucked back by the tide. The continuous motion of the waves was mesmerising, breaking and retreating, breaking and retreating, and the accompanying cry of seagulls carried away on the wind added to the soundtrack of Will's life.

'I just miss it, Mum.'

'Are you happy in London, Will?'

'Yes, I think so. I've got a good job, a nice house, Rachel and the boys. What more could a man want?' He gave Pippa a weak smile.

'Yes, but does that make you happy? You're still so young. Since Dad had his heart attack, he's been worrying about whether he pressurised you to go into the bank and move to London and he's rethinking the whole thing now, given what's happened to him. He doesn't want you ending up as stressed with work as he was.'

'Does he think that's what caused it then, stress?'

'Well things have definitely got more pressured over the past few years and the doctors seem to think stress can have a lot to do with it.'

'Well, it's a bit late for me now, isn't it? I can hardly leave the bank, with a family to support. And Rach would never move to Cornwall anyway.' He hoped he didn't sound bitter.

'And are you and Rachel happy together?' Pippa asked gently, linking Will's arm.

'Yes of course,' he replied tightly. 'We're fine mum. Look, I don't want you and Dad to be worrying about me.' But was he happy with Rachel? He tried to sweep away the confusion he felt when he asked himself that question; it was easier than confronting it. 'Come on, let's catch up with the others.' They scrambled across the beach towards Seth, Dan (who had Mikey on his shoulders), and the twins.

'Oh by the way, Tam was asking after you the other day. She'd love to see you while you're here.' Was that a knowing look she gave Will? He coloured slightly and strode on towards the rest of the family.

***

Will woke late on Sunday morning. Evie and Grace had taken charge of Mikey to give Will a lie-in, and he'd made the most of it. He came downstairs to find Dan and Seth at the kitchen table with cups of coffee and the newspapers. Pippa was just putting a huge joint of beef in the oven. 'Hope we're having yorkies with that, Mum,' he said, as he planted a kiss on her cheek before pouring himself a coffee and joining his brother and father.

'Of course,' she replied. 'Dan, can you peel the potatoes please?'

'Where's Mikey?' Will asked.

'The girls have taken him out in his pushchair, but I don't think they'll get far before it rains. Why don't you go and meet them? They've gone down to the harbour.'

'Yes okay. You coming, Dan?'

'No, looks like I'm peeling spuds!'

'Being the absent son does have its advantages. I get to enjoy all the perks but I'm no longer on the chores rota!'

'Sod off Will!' Dan laughed. He grabbed a tea towel and tried to flick it across the back of Will's legs, but Will dodged it just in time.

'Still faster than you! See you later.' Will grabbed an old Barbour coat hanging in the boot room and launched himself into a windy Cornish morning. He strode along Mount's Road, a narrow street set above the beach and between tiny fishermen's cottages, some of which, he noticed, had been done up and turned into holiday homes. Soon he reached the Porthleven Institute building, with its distinctive clock tower, and walked out to the end of the breakwater, tasting the salty air on his lips. His heart swelled, like the waters below him, for this small corner of Cornwall where lives and livelihoods have, for thousands of years, been inextricably linked to the forces of nature, to the vagaries of the sea. For many, it was still a tough way of life, but a colourful one. A grey job, in a grey suit, in a grey bank was no substitute. With a heavy sigh he pointed his face into the buffeting wind and closed his eyes.

'Will!' He turned at the sound of his name, looking for the twins and Mikey, but there was no sign of them walking along Harbour Road. Instead, Tam was hurrying towards him. 'Will, I thought it was you!' She ran along the breakwater and into his arms.

'Tam. So good to see you. Have you seen Evie and Grace?' Will asked, without letting her go.

Eventually, they moved apart. 'Yes, they've gone back through the village. They asked me to lunch, d'you think Pippa will mind? I was just going to pop home and change but saw you out here. Are you getting some fresh Cornish air?'

'Of course she won't mind. You should've seen the size of the joint she put in the oven. She always cooks like she's feeding the entire Porthleven fishing fleet!'

They stood together, Will's arms across Tam's shoulder, and watched the powerful breakers crashing on to the shore, each with a thunderous boom greater than the one before. The force of the unrelenting sea could still move Will to the depths of his soul. He shuddered and held Tam tighter.

'How have you been? Everything alright in the big bad city? Isn't Mikey gorgeous and the spitting image of you? Does Matty look like you too?'

'Alright, yes, yes and yes! Does that answer your questions? And yes, they are both gorgeous, just like me!'

Tam punched Will playfully on the arm. 'Don't go getting above yourself, city boy!'

Will became more serious. 'I'm glad I came down. I wanted to see how Dad is doing, and he seems to be making a great recovery, so it's put my mind at rest. God only knows when I'll get back again. Rachel is less than keen so it'll probably be next summer. I just miss it all so much.'

Tam turned to face Will and looked up into his eyes. 'Will –' she began, but before she could say more, he bent towards her and kissed her softly on her lips. She responded with a small gasp but didn't pull away and they held one another in a tight embrace.

'I'm sorry Tam,' whispered Will into her hair, 'I couldn't help it.'

'Oh Will,' she said, and she kissed him again. And then it started pelting down with rain.

'Come on, let's go,' said Will, and took Tam's hand as they raced from the breakwater and back along Cliff Road.

'Look what the cat's brought in, a drowned rat!' said Will as he and Tam dripped their way into the warm kitchen.

'Will, don't be so rude to Tam!' said Pippa. 'Tam, you're welcome as always. Evie said she'd asked you to join us. The more the merrier.'

'Thanks Pippa. I found him on the breakwater, wasn't sure if he'd still remember the way home so thought I'd better bring him!'

***

After a massive lunch, accompanied by a very good red wine, Dan decided it was time to play Twister. Everyone groaned but he wasn't to be thwarted. 'Come on, you need to work off that lunch.'

'I'm more likely to puke it up,' said Grace, but she helped him unfold the plastic sheet with the coloured circles. 'We haven't played this for ages; I think it was the Christmas before you went away Will.'

'All the more reason to play it again then, come on!'

In a few minutes they were tangled together in impossible poses, squealing as they tried to maintain their balance. And then Mikey toddled into the middle of the game and tried to climb on to Will's back. The game collapsed and everyone landed in a heap on top of one another, shrieking with laughter. Dan extricated himself first, as the phone rang.

'Oh, hi Rachel. Yeah, Will's just here on the floor, tangled up with Tam.'

Chapter 11
2016

Lucy woke to a beam of sunlight stealing its way through a chink in the curtains, right into her eyes. Something felt different about her bed, and she realised it was Jake lying beside her. Suddenly memories of the night before came into focus. They'd fallen asleep on the sofa and woken up sometime later to Ronnie Barker waxing on about four candles, or was it fork handles? – the telly was still streaming 1970s comedy classics. They stretched and groaned, and Jake turned off the TV.

'Don't leave me tonight, Jake,' Lucy said. 'Please stay.'

Jake kissed her gently. 'If you're sure, I don't want to take advantage ….'

'I'm sure,' and she led him upstairs. Now she lay next to Jake's sleeping form and a smile played on her lips at the memory of their first time together. With that, Jake stirred and gave a contented sigh.

'Morning gorgeous,' he said. 'Is it too early to tell you I've fallen in love with you?'

'Too early in the morning or too early in our relationship? Whatever, no it isn't because it's reciprocated!' With that, they snuggled up together and cocooned themselves under the duvet.

***

Two hours later they were back at the dining table with a cafetière of coffee and two mugs, ready to tackle the bundle of letters. Lucy had a feeling of déjà vu.

'Here goes,' she said, taking the first one from the pile and easing it out of the dog-eared envelope, which was stamped with an unreadable postmark. The letter was addressed to a PO Box number. She read aloud to Jake.

15 Osbourne Terrace
Eastbourne
July '84

Dear Mrs Askwith

As we agreed, I am writing to let you know about Rachel. She has been staying here with us for a while but has now found a place of her own. It's not much, but we hope it will be a start for her to get back on her feet. Thank you for your financial support towards the flat.

As agreed, she does not know I am in touch with you.

Simon and I will continue to support her as best we can.

I hope Lucy is thriving.

Best wishes

Becky Brown

Lucy's hands were shaking. 'Lucy? Oh God, that's me! What happened? This is only three months after I was born. Did Rachel have some sort of breakdown, is that why I was with Susannah and George? And why is she in Eastbourne? My birth certificate said I was born in London.'

'I don't know,' said Jake gently. 'Do you want to carry on?'

Lucy didn't reply and picked up the next letter in the bundle.

15 Osbourne Terrace
Eastbourne
Jan '85

Dear Mrs Askwith

We agreed I would write every six months. Since my last letter Rachel settled into her flat and found a job as a typist, which she seemed to enjoy. She was doing so well and, until Christmas, swore she was sober. But the festive season has been very difficult for her, and her old habits got the better of her. However, she has agreed to attend Alcoholics Anonymous again, and we are praying that this time it will do the trick.

I still hope, one day, that you may be reconciled.

I hope Lucy continues to thrive.

Best wishes

Becky Brown

Lucy was crying now, silent tears trickling down her face. She passed the letter to Jake and picked up the last one in the pile.

15 Osbourne Terrace

Eastbourne

July '85

Dear Mrs Askwith

I am so sorry to write with such sad news, but Rachel passed away two weeks ago, on 3rd July. She was found in her flat by the police. I gave them your box number so I assume they have contacted you, but as I haven't heard from them, or you, and have no 'phone number, I thought I should let you know in case you haven't been notified.

I take it you will let Will know.

We will miss Rachel; she had a good heart but, in the end, couldn't fight her demons.

I am enclosing the most recent photo I have of Rach, with me, taken a short while ago.

I am so sorry. I won't be in touch with you again.

Becky Brown

'Oh no,' Lucy whispered, and her tears turned to sobs. 'Poor Rachel. Poor Susannah.' Jake held her as her body shook, wracked with grief for the mother she had never known, and for the woman she had believed was her mother, both gone from this world. After a while, when there were no more tears left to cry, Lucy sat in a sort of trance, her mind numb, unable to process anything more. Jake poured them both a coffee. 'Well, that's it. Now I know. My mother died a drunk,' Lucy said bitterly. 'So much for Susannah saying *it may open doors to love for you and Daisy, from others that you should have known.* Why would she say that when she already knew my mother was dead? It's so cruel.' Lucy was angry now; angry at the injustice of having been brought up, unknowingly, part of this tragic story. She was angry for Daisy too, both of them having inadvertently lived a lie.

'It does seem cruel Lucy, and desperately sad about your mum, but maybe there are other family members, your father for instance, who might still be out there somewhere.'

'And how the hell are we supposed to find him if he is? She didn't exactly leave many clues, did she?'

'No, she didn't.' Jake was quiet for a moment, not wanting to push Lucy, but hoping to help her channel her anger into something more constructive. 'I know you need time to process all this, but maybe you could start with trying to find Becky Brown. She must've known Rachel very well and might be able to help you piece together what happened.'

'You're right,' said Lucy, sniffing loudly. 'I'm just frightened of being let down all over again; what happens if we can't find her? She may be dead too for all we know, and then what?'

Jake was encouraged to hear Lucy refer to 'we' – he wanted to be beside her in her quest for answers and it seems she was thinking of them as one. 'I don't know, but if you want to try and find answers it seems like the only place to start.'

'I just don't know what a Pandora's box I may be opening but, you're right, I can't leave it now. Oh heavens, have I even got the energy for all this?'

'You're stronger than you think, Lucy. Look at what you've coped with so far. And, to use another metaphor, I'll be with you, whatever can of worms we open.'

Lucy's mind's eye suddenly conjured up a ridiculous image of worms bursting out of a baked bean can and tangling themselves in Pandora's hair, while she tried to free them and put them in her box. She started to laugh uncontrollably, and then Jake was laughing too until the two of them were wiping tears of hilarity from their eyes. And in that moment, as she felt the simple joy of laughter again, she knew, with Jake by her side, she would be able to get through this.

***

By mid-afternoon they had formulated a vague plan. Jake was due to return to Cornwall and needed to see his parents before he left, as well as call at the gallery in Tunbridge Wells displaying his art. The new school term was edging ever closer for Lucy, and she knew, once it started, her time for sleuthing would be limited.

'Why don't we both have a go at finding out what we can about this Becky Brown online and then, if we get any leads in Eastbourne, we could take a trip there? I could manage a weekend sometime if you could get there for a day,' suggested Jake.

'We may as well start there, I suppose; we've got nothing else to go on. It's just such a big step.'

'Not as big as the ones you've taken in the last few days, and I'll be with you all the way. Come here lovely Lucy.' Jake pulled Lucy to him and they stood entwined, neither wanting to let go. Eventually they drew apart. 'I'm going to have to go sweetheart, although it breaks me to leave you. Will you be okay?'

'Yes, I think so. Daisy will be back soon, so I'll have to be. I think I'll tell her about Rachel's death and show her the photos and then leave it, unless she's got any questions. Then I'm going to try and enjoy the rest of the summer with her and allow myself just a couple of hours an evening for investigating.' Lucy was good at compartmentalising; it was how she'd survived her chaotic childhood. Maybe it would be a good skill to see her through what was to come.

***

About half an hour after Jake left, Daisy came barrelling through the door, followed by Emily and Chloe. Lucy had shed more tears as she waved Jake off, unsure of when they would be together again, but as soon as Daisy started describing what she and Emily had been up to – including a trip to a friend of Chloe's to see some newborn kittens – she couldn't help but get carried along with her enthusiasm.

After a quick cup of tea, and squash for the girls, Chloe and Emily left. Daisy came and cuddled up to Lucy on the sofa.

'What have you been doing Mum? Is Jake still here?'

'No, Jake went a little while ago, he's going back to Cornwall.'

'Lucky him.'

'Yes indeed. He was really helpful though, and we started going through some papers that Granny (your Great Granny) left for me.'

'Oh. What were they?'

'Well, there were some photos and some letters and legal papers. I'll show you the photos in a minute. You remember when you asked if my real mummy had died? Well, she had. She died when I was a baby and I think that's why Granny brought me up.'

'But why did she say she was your mum when she wasn't?'

'Maybe so I wouldn't be sad that my mum had died. It wasn't really the right thing to do, but sometimes we do things because we think we're helping, without thinking of the consequences.'

Daisy was quiet for a moment, a deep frown over her pretty brown eyes. 'Is that like when you don't own up to something you've done wrong, but then you get found out anyway and get into even more trouble, because you didn't tell the truth in the first place?'

'Yes, I suppose it is, something like that.'

'That happened to Billy at school. He pushed Mia over in the playground and then ran away. She didn't see who pushed her, but she broke her arm. When everyone was asked who did it, no one owned up, but the next day Jamie told Mrs Graves that he'd seen Billy do it. Jamie got into trouble for not telling Mrs Graves straight away and Billy got into even more trouble for breaking Mia's arm. And then we all got this long lecture from Mr Williams in assembly the next day, something about tangled spiders' webs and lying.'

Lucy laughed. "Oh, what a tangled web we weave when once we practise to deceive."

'Yes, that's it! How did you know?'

'It's an old saying which means more or less what we were talking about.'

'Oh. Can I see the photos now?'

They studied the photos together, Daisy examining them closely while Lucy explained who she thought they were. 'I don't know who the little boys are, or Will, but Becky was my mum's friend. There is still a lot we need to find out.'

'How will you do that?'

'Well, Jake and I are going to be doing a bit of investigating, like detectives.'

'Oh wow, can I help?'

'You can when we get some leads. But Jake's going to start by searching online.'

That didn't seem quite so appealing to Daisy. 'Oh okay. What are we doing tomorrow?'

'Well, Ellie had her baby yesterday so I'm hoping we can go and visit tomorrow. She's had a little girl called Lyra.'

'Like in *His Dark Materials*? Cool!'

'Well, I'm not sure they named her after *that* Lyra, but it is a pretty name.'

Lucy and Daisy spent a cosy evening together watching *Moana*, singing along enthusiastically to the uplifting songs, and Lucy felt her spirits rise. Later, once Daisy was settled in bed, Lucy gathered up the photos and papers and put them in a folder for safekeeping. On her way to bed, she went to close the safe in Susannah's bedroom, which she and Jake had abandoned when they moved the documents downstairs. She knelt down and reached into the cupboard and saw another photo in the bottom of the safe. It must have slipped out of the pack, she thought, as she lifted it out. She read the caption on the back first – Anna, George, Rachel, Will, Evie, Mikey and Matty, Cornwall 1983 – and gasped as she turned it over and saw them all standing in front of Cornwall Castle. She ran downstairs and grabbed the framed photo of Susannah and George in exactly the same spot, then scrolled through her phone to those she had taken in Cornwall, and there it was again, the same imposing property, Daisy's make-believe Cornwall Castle.

What does it all mean? Lucy asked herself. Who are these people with my so-called parents and my birth mother? Why is Susannah noted as Anna on the photo? This is less than two years before I was born – what the hell happened between this picture being taken and my birth, to change the course of all these lives?

Chapter 12

1982/83

'Hi Rach, everything okay?' asked Will, with a forced brightness.

'Well, I was just ringing to find out how things are going with your dad, but obviously *you're* having a great time 'tangled up' with Tam. Bloody hell Will, what's going on? Every time you go to Cornwall, I catch you cosying up with her. So much for the concerned son returning to minister to his ailing dad.'

'I knew you'd take it the wrong way. We, and by that, I mean *all* of us, were having a game of Twister. Hardly cosying up.'

'Twister? From what I remember, it was just an excuse to get up close and personal.'

'What, with my brother and sisters? For God's sake Rach.'

'Brother, sisters *and* Tam. How convenient!'

'She's more like another sister, that's all.' But he knew she wasn't. 'Mikey joined in too and tried to climb on my back and the whole thing collapsed,' he added, trying to lighten the mood. 'Anyway, how's Matty? And did you have a good night out with the girls?'

Now it was Rachel's turn to sound cagey. 'Yeah, great. Mum and Dad had Matty at theirs and I stayed with Becky. We went to Blitz, it was jumping!'

'I won't ask how sozzled you got. Did you break any new records?' Will tried to ask teasingly, but it sounded critical, even to him.

'There you go again. Listen, if you will leave me here while you go off to your beloved Cornwall, I have to make my own entertainment.'

Will was about to retort with, 'Well you could've come with me' but the fight had gone out of him. 'Look, can we drop this?' he said instead. 'Dad is doing really well; Mikey and I will be home tomorrow.' He was aware that he was on the phone in the hall and the family was in the living room on the other side of the wall. Someone had at least closed the door on their conversation. Will was still cursing Dan for innocently dropping him in it again, but Dan was so guileless, he would never intentionally do or say anything to cause trouble. Was Will's sensitivity towards Dan's tactlessness because of his own reignited feelings for Tam?

***

Will and Mikey left first thing in the morning, Will's heart heavy at leaving Porthleven and his family. He tried to convince himself it wasn't because he was already missing Tam. After seven long hours on the road, fighting with his conscience, he had persuaded himself that he must focus on the wellbeing of his own family, put more effort into making a life for them in London, help Rachel tackle the demon drink that seemed to have a hold on her and be the kind of father to his boys that his own was to him. Rachel's more than cool reception, when he arrived home with a tired and grumpy Mikey, nearly weakened his resolve, but Matty, who was obviously ecstatic to have his daddy home – squirming out of Rachel's arms and into his with a 'Dadda, Dadda, Dadda!' – restored his determination at once.

A fragile truce existed between Rachel and Will in the run up to Christmas. Rachel was all consumed with the playgroup party and Will was up to his neck at work. Mikey, now heading towards three years old, was picking up on the buzz of the Christmas build-up and was continually over excited, while Matty had just started toddling and was like a miniature tornado. With two demanding toddlers and exhausting schedules, there was little time to dwell on the state of their relationship. The one positive for Will was that Rachel was off the booze and had adopted the role of 'pillar of the playgroup'.

Rachel's parents, Anna and George, joined the family for Christmas Day, which was a happy occasion with only a limited amount of alcohol. The boys were given far too many presents and enjoyed playing in the boxes more than with the toys themselves.

'We could've saved ourselves a fortune,' said Will, 'and just picked up some empty boxes from the supermarket. They would've been just as happy!'

'Good point Will, we'll remember that next year,' replied George.

'Talking of next year, why don't we all go on holiday together?' said Rachel, suddenly. 'It would be good fun wouldn't it and the boys would love it?'

'Where did that come from, Rach?' asked Will in surprise.

A look passed between Anna and George, Anna uncharitably thinking they were only being asked along as unpaid babysitters. 'Are you sure? What d'you think George?'

George, ever the peacekeeper, nodded his agreement. 'I don't see why not? Do you get any say in this Will?' he asked, sensing Will's astonishment at Rachel's request.

'Probably not, but you know what they say, 'a happy wife is a happy life', so I'll go along with it! Just so long as we can go to Cornwall. Mum and Dad haven't met Matty yet and they're longing to see him. And you can meet them too,' he added, to Anna and George.

Rachel was about to issue a groan – she'd been hoping for a trip to Spain at least – when Anna piped up, 'I'd like to see Cornwall, we've never been, have we George? And we really ought to meet your parents, Will.'

'We won't stay with them though, it would be too much for them,' said Rachel quickly. 'Let's see if we can find a place nearby. Will, you must know of somewhere.'

'I certainly know where *not* to go! I'm sure Mum will be able to recommend something.' He thought it ridiculous to be going to Cornwall and not stay at his family home but, although they had a large house, it wouldn't accommodate all of them so there was no choice. At least, he thought, with Anna and George along, Rach should stay off the drink and it would help with the kids.

***

January was a flat month, as it so often is. After the busyness of the Christmas party and the kudos that came with its success, Rachel felt at a bit of a loss with nothing and no-one to organise. Michael and Matty both caught colds which made them grouchy and snotty. There was no let up at the bank for Will and the winter blues settled on him in the hard grey city; no vast stormy skies and turbulent seas that made him feel so alive; no walks along the rugged coast to Loe Bar, seagulls calling with their mournful cries, to blow the cobwebs away in the wild, Cornish winter. He rarely saw daylight, leaving for work and returning home in the dark, and longed for the comfort of The Ship Inn, huddled round the fire with his mates, or the solace of his thin place. His thoughts drifted all too frequently to Tam, and the resulting guilt did nothing to improve his mood.

Will was increasingly worried about Rachel's drinking, despite a bold announcement that she was giving up for the whole of January. It lasted about a week before Will caught the sickly smell of alcohol on her breath. She denied it, of course, and had become adept at hiding her habit (no empty bottles in the bin or dirty glasses on the drainer). But Will knew he had to have it out with her and that the mother of all rows would undoubtedly ensue. He waited until he had put Mikey and Matty to bed then braced himself for another fight.

'What happened to no drinking in January?' asked Will, when he sat down next to Rachel who was slumped on the sofa. 'Fallen off the wagon already?'

Immediately, Rachel was on the defensive. 'No, of course not. What makes you say that?'

'D'you think I'm stupid? I can smell it on your breath. You might at least clean your teeth if you want to fool me. How much have you had?'

'Look, I just fancied a little tipple. I bought a bottle of wine at the off licence on the way home from playgroup, that's all.'

'What? And drank the lot? Bloody hell, what about the boys?'

'No, they didn't want any!' Rachel started to giggle.

'That isn't even funny, Rachel.'

'Ooh, you must be cross, you called me Rachel.' Suddenly she was contrite. 'I'm sorry, Will. I was feeling a bit down, you know, just needed a pick me up. I didn't have much and you know I can hold it.' It was true, for the most part she could drink an alarming amount without it affecting her, and she functioned as well as she needed to so as not to draw attention to herself. 'I'll be a good girl from now on, promise.' She leant in and kissed Will. 'Don't be cross with me,' she pleaded in a whinging voice. 'I won't drink again until our next night out with the gang.'

'If only I could believe you,' sighed Will, with a heavy heart. He was fearful of saying the word 'alcoholic' out loud to Rachel, because that might make it true, but it gnawed away at him, like an aching tooth.

Rachel heaved herself off the sofa. 'Of course you can believe me,' she simpered, then added suggestively, 'I'm going for a soak in the bath now, are you going to join me?'

'No, you're all right.' Rachel sauntered off and Will was appalled at how sickened he felt by the mother of his children.

Luckily, nights out with the gang were less frequent – no one had much spare cash at this time of year – but when they did hit the town, Rachel led the way in the drinking games and high jinks as usual. Will was losing his taste for this way of life and, if he hadn't needed to keep an eye on Rachel, would quite happily have stayed home with the boys. As it was, Anna continued to babysit, Rachel continued to suffer raging hangovers and Will pined for his beloved Cornwall. At least Mikey and Matty, once over their winter colds, continued to thrive, for which Will was grateful.

***

By February the idea of a family holiday together had been settled and a country house hotel a few miles from Porthleven was chosen – Anna and George were generously picking up the bill.

'As far as Mum knows it has a good reputation and it's right above a small cove which doesn't get busy. Most of the Emmets go to Praa Sands,' said Will disdainfully. 'It'll be great for taking the boys rock pooling.'

'Who are the Emmets?' asked Rachel, puzzled.

Will laughed. 'It's what we call holidaymakers. It's an old Cornish word for an ant and, believe me, it's like being invaded by an army of ants when it gets busy in the summer!'

'You make it sound charming. I don't know why I didn't insist we go to Spain.'

***

February slipped into March and the hope of Spring was in the air. Will's winter blues lifted with the changing season and Rachel once again found herself at the helm of the playgroup committee, this time with the task of organising the Easter Bonnet parade. She was determined it would be the best one yet. Will allowed himself a glimmer of hope that her creativity, enthusiasm and confidence in this project would propel her away from the demon drink. With Will's mood improving and Rachel launching herself into another worthwhile cause, a closeness they hadn't known for some time crept back into their lives.

It was a Saturday evening; Mikey and Matty were in their pyjamas, cuddled up with Will on the sofa for a story, while Rachel put the finishing touches to the bonnets they had all had a hand in making (which really meant trimming up the random pieces of coloured paper the boys had enthusiastically stuck to the hats). Tissue paper and glue was everywhere, the kitchen table a sticky mess.

'Right boys, here they are!' announced Rachel, as she entered with a bonnet in each hand. 'Come and try them on.' The boys scrambled off the sofa, the story forgotten, as they pulled at Rachel's legs to reach the finished creations.

'Hang on,' said Will coming to the rescue. 'Right Mikey, here's yours, let's see how it looks.' He placed it on Mikey's head as he squealed with excitement.

'Let me see, let me see!' he shouted, feeling the bonnet atop his head. Will lifted him up to show him in the mirror above the fireplace. 'I can see the chicks and the eggs!' he giggled.

'Chicks, eggs!' repeated Matty, as he too was hoisted up to admire his bonnet.

'Don't they look sweet?' said Rachel proudly. 'They can't really win though, can they, with me being on the committee?'

'Don't see why not,' replied Will. 'You won't be on the judging panel, so it won't be up to you. *We* know theirs will be the best anyway and that's all that matters.' He gave Rachel a hug and a kiss as the children paraded up and down the living room. 'Well done you.'

Later, once the bonnets were safely stored away, after a bit of a fight from Matty who insisted he wanted to wear his to bed, Rachel and Will cleared up the mess in the kitchen and settled in to watch *Blind Date*, hosted by Cilla Black getting a 'lorra lorra laughs'. They snuggled up together and Will felt the shudder of desire he'd known when, in the early days, they'd spent whole afternoons in bed together. He lifted Rachel into his arms and carried her up to bed.

***

The Easter parade was a huge success and, because Rachel was on an even keel, so was life for the rest of the family. It seemed the rollercoaster that was Rachel's life had come to a rest, for now at least. And so it was that when they left for the much-anticipated holiday in May, Will had high hopes for Rachel coming to love his home county and, more importantly, stay off the alcohol.

The Castle Country House Hotel was, as Will had promised, set on the cliffs above a path leading directly to a small rocky cove. Once rooms were allocated and bags unpacked, Will announced he was taking the boys to the beach. 'Are you coming, Mummy?' he said to Rachel, hoping she'd be as keen as him to show the children their natural playground for the next week.

'No, I'll stay here and sort things out, have a look round the hotel. I said we'd meet Mum and Dad in the lounge.'

'Okay, see you there later, come on boys. Let's go and see the sea!'

Chapter 13
2016

'Lucy, my dear girl, Edward here. How are you? Have you found out any more about Becky's whereabouts? Is there anything we can do to help?'

'Edward, it's so good to hear from you. How's Charles? Is he getting over his cataract operation?'

'Oh yes, he's fine but he is *the* most awful patient. He makes the *biggest* fuss when I put the eyedrops in and I have to do it four times a day! Honestly, I'm exhausted! We're thinking of going to the flat in Eastbourne for a few days to recuperate, and I think I need more convalescence than he does!'

'Perhaps he's just getting his own back from when you had your knee done; I seem to remember much the same comments from him at the time!'

'Yes, well, the less said about that the better. Anyway, how are things with you?'

Lucy filled Edward in on the somewhat fruitless online searches she and Jake had attempted, in trying to trace Becky Brown in Eastbourne. Neither of them had been able to devote much time to their investigations; since the new school term started, Lucy had little time for anything that wasn't connected to supporting two autistic children in year three and running Daisy to after school activities (swimming, drama and seemingly endless invitations to tea). Jake had been given the opportunity to sell his art out of a gallery in Porthleven and was frantically getting his pieces sale ready (finishing, mounting and framing).

'... so it's been a bit full on Edward, and we've decided just to go to Eastbourne and call at the address on the letters. D'you think it's a bonkers idea? It's certainly a long shot but I don't want to leave any stone unturned.'

'You must do what you think is best, my dear. And I insist that you and Jake use the flat – that's what it's there for, after all. We keep intending to spend more time there ourselves, but you know how it is. I say, why don't we all go at the same time, then we can do something with Daisy while you and Jake look for clues.'

Lucy laughed. 'You make us sound like Sherlock Holmes and Miss Marple, but it would be wonderful to stay at the flat, thank you so much. We're planning to go next weekend; Daisy will be away on a school trip, so we thought we'd take the opportunity. Will that fit with you?'

'Oh yes, we can go whenever suits. Let's say we'll see you there on the Friday evening. Charles will be beside himself to show it off to you!'

***

After seeing Daisy on to the coach for the year six school journey to the Isle of Wight – 'it's alright, you can go now Mum, it's not cool to hang about waiting for us to leave' – Lucy had a fraught day with year three. It seemed the departure of the year six class had excited the rest of the school, making the children particularly raucous and noisy. As soon as school was over, she'd driven to Tonbridge station to meet Jake, who had chosen to come by train, rather than endure another endless drive from one end of the country to the other. They'd travelled straight on to Eastbourne and eventually pulled up outside the prestigious block of flats where Edward and Charles had bought a penthouse apartment less than a year ago, in the Sovereign Harbour area of the seaside town. Lucy had a sudden memory of Suzannah commenting on how swish it looked when they'd shown her the details, but had quickly gone on to comment that she didn't understand why they needed to be so close to the sea. She shrugged off the memory and concentrated on the feelings stirring inside her, with Jake by her side again. And then Charles and Edward were striding towards them across the parking area.

'My dears, how lovely to see you. We're so glad you could come and share some time with us at our darling little bolthole. Do come in and see it.' Charles was gushing, and after hugs all round, they travelled up to the top floor in the lift.

'Wow!' gasped Lucy, as she stepped into a large airy living room with a wall of glass doors leading to a balcony, overlooking the marina. 'This is amazing!' Charles was a successful interior design consultant, and she knew the apartment would be up to the minute in décor, but this was a whole other level.

Charles beamed at Lucy's reaction and waved his arms affectedly. 'It is rather special, isn't it? Come and sit in the Egg chair, you get the *best* views from here.' Lucy dutifully took a seat in the retro oval shaped chair suspended in a chrome frame, and for a moment was transported back to Cornwall, as the strong coastal light streamed in through the windows.

'This is some place,' said Jake, seeing it with an architect's eye. 'A great use of space,' he added, as he surveyed the generous proportions of the kitchen/dining/living room.

'We love it, but haven't really used it as much as we thought we would. However, we are planning to rectify that, starting right now, aren't we Charles?' Edward looked at his husband lovingly.

'Oh yes indeed, and we are honoured that you are our first guests. And to celebrate we are taking you out to dinner. No, I don't want any arguments, our treat, we insist!'

Over a superb meal in a top-class restaurant, Lucy and Jake explained their plans for the weekend, which really only amounted to one full day, as they had to return to their opposite ends of the country on Sunday. 'Tomorrow we're going to go and knock on the door of 15 Osbourne Terrace and see what happens. I'm sure we must be mad, but who knows? We've got to start somewhere,' said

Lucy, feeling rather hopeless at the likelihood of her mother's friend of thirty years ago still living there.

Jake sensed the shift in her disposition and took her hand. 'It'll be okay Lucy, and if we don't get anywhere, we can search electoral registers and the like. Most people are traceable these days.'

'Well, we wish you all the luck in the world and will help however we can,' said Edward.

'Let's drink to that,' said Charles, and they raised their glasses to what lay ahead.

***

Lucy awoke before Jake and immediately felt comforted by his presence next to her. She lay still, watching him sleep, thinking of their tender lovemaking the night before. Edward and Charles had tactfully taken themselves off once they'd arrived back at the apartment and left Lucy and Jake to their own devices. They had been given a bedroom with magnificent views over the marina and a state-of-the-art en-suite. 'Better than a five-star hotel,' Jake had commented, before falling back on the bed, pulling Lucy with him.

Now Lucy stood at the window looking out over the sea, wondering when she would find the answers to the questions that haunted her. Would today be the start of a journey of discovery or another dead-end? Jake awoke, stretched, yawned and came to stand beside her. 'Nice view,' he said, 'but not Cornwall. There's something so unique about the Cornish light that I've never found anywhere else. Anyway, no time for dawdling and daydreaming this morning. We're on a mission Miss Marple, come on!'

After showering and a quick breakfast of coffee and croissants, Jake checked the map on his phone for directions to Osbourne Terrace. 'It's about a half hour walk if we go along the seafront. Shall we blow the cobwebs away, it's a fine morning?'

They left a note for Edward and Charles (who had not yet surfaced) and set off along the prom, the shelving shingly beach on one side, guesthouses and hotels on the other. They were tempted to detour onto the pier but continued along the front, past the iconic bandstand and well-manicured gardens. It was a bright early autumn day, the sky an uninterrupted azure, the warmth of the sun giving the impression that summer hadn't quite given up just yet. Lucy and Jake strode along hand in hand, stealing kisses when they stopped to watch the comings and goings on the beach. Eventually, they turned inland and were soon outside number 15 Osbourne Terrace, an attractive terraced house in a well-cared for row of identical homes. Lucy nearly lost her resolve. 'I don't know about this Jake. Are you sure we should be here?'

'Well, I don't know about you, but I haven't come all this way to chicken out now. If it's not the right house, we just apologise and walk away, simple!' And with that, he walked up to the front door and rang the bell. They both held their breath until they heard footsteps approaching along a hard floor, and the door opened.

'Hello?' said the young woman who stood in the doorway.

'Oh hi,' said Jake, after looking at Lucy and realising she was seemingly struck dumb. 'We're looking for a Becky Brown who lived here in the 1980s.'

The woman smiled. 'Sorry, we've only been here since 2010 I don't think it was Brown who was here before but to be honest I can't remember.'

Lucy couldn't help but gasp 'Oh no,' as she felt her world tumble around her again.

'Oh okay, sorry to have disturbed you,' said Jake, feeling deflated. They turned to walk away but the woman, seeing the disappointment on their faces, piped up again.

'I tell you what, we could ask Dot next door. She's been here forever and knows everyone. I'm sure she won't mind, but I'll come with you, I don't want to worry her.' They followed the woman to number 17, and she unlocked the door herself, calling to Dot as she went in. 'Dot, can I come in, it's Julie?' She looked back at Jake and

Lucy and asked them to wait on the doorstep. A moment later, Julie returned with a spritely looking older woman, smartly dressed in a tweed skirt and twinset, pearls at her neck. Miss Marple herself, thought Lucy. Jake took the lead again; introduced them and said they were looking for Becky Brown. Suddenly Lucy found her voice again. 'I think Becky Brown was a friend of my mother's and I'm trying to trace her. Not my mother, she died, but Becky because she knew her and I didn't. I was brought up by my grandmother.' She realised she was rambling and not making much sense, so stopped.

Dot scrutinised Lucy for a moment, her brow furrowed. 'Why don't you come in, I think I may be able to help you. Julie, will you stay too? Just in case they're a couple of ne'er do wells trying to scam me out of my life savings,' she said laughingly, with a twinkle in her eye.

'Oh, thank you,' said Lucy. 'We're not here to cause you any alarm.'

'Come on dear, in we go.' Dot led the way into a neat sitting room, furnished in a surprisingly contemporary style; pale blue sofas, with contrasting navy cushions and candy-stripe throws adding a splash of colour. 'Please sit down. Now, shall we all have a cup of tea?'

'I'll make it,' said Julie. 'You stay here Dot.'

'She's such a dear,' said Dot to Lucy and Jake. 'She pops round every day to make sure I'm alright. And her children are so polite. Now, let me see how I can help you.'

***

Over a cup of tea and a plate of biscuits, Dot explained how she'd come to know Becky and her husband Simon when they moved next door in the early 80's. 'Becky was expecting Hannah at the time. Such a bonny baby, and then they went on to have Peter about two years later. They are a lovely family and became like my own. I never married, you see, so they sort of adopted me as a surrogate grandmother and vice versa.'

'You said they *are* a lovely family. Are you still in touch? Did they move far away?' asked Lucy cautiously.

'Oh yes dear, I see them regularly. They're still in Eastbourne and I'll give you their address in a minute. You see, I think I remember your mother. Becky was such a good friend to her and helped her when she was down on her luck. I wish I could remember her name.'

'Rachel,' said Lucy, her heart thumping. 'Did you know her, what was she like?'

'Ah yes, that's it. I didn't really know her but met her a few times when she was staying with Becky. She was very, um, troubled.' She gave Lucy a sympathetic smile. 'Becky and Simon did so much for her, but in the end, it became too much, especially with the little ones around….' Dot suddenly seemed at a loss as to what to say. 'I think you should talk with Becky, I'm sure she'd love to hear from you. She was so devastated when Rachel died. I'm sorry my dear, this must be very hard for you.' Lucy was looking down, wringing her hands and trying not to cry.

Jake, sitting next to her, put his arm around her shoulders. 'Thank you for telling us what you know, Dot,' he said softly. 'I think, as you suggest, we will speak to Becky. Lucy is so desperate to find out more about her mother. You said you have her address?'

Dot went to her desk and fumbled about for a bit, then passed Jake a piece of paper with an Eastbourne address and phone number. 'Here it is. I'm sure she won't mind me passing it on to you and I hope you find what you're looking for my dear.'

As they were leaving Lucy gave Dot a hug. 'Thank you, you've been so kind.'

'Oh, that's alright dear. You know, you've got a look of your mother – I think it's the shape of your face. I remember how pretty she was.'

Lucy gave a watery smile, and they said their goodbyes, leaving Julie and Dot clearing away the tea things.

***

As soon as they were a few steps away from Dot's house, Lucy dissolved into tears and into Jake's arms. 'I don't know if I'm crying from sadness or relief,' she said, half sobbing and half laughing. 'Knowing that Dot met my mum, it's just incredible, and that she's given us Becky's address. I don't think I really believed it would happen.'

'Well, it is happening, sweetheart. Are you ready for the next step?'

'Yes, but let's get a coffee somewhere first. I need to reset, and we can check where the house is.'

They found a café where they took stock, chewed over their meeting with Dot and gathered themselves, before making their way to The Firs on Westleigh Avenue. The house was aptly named – tall pine trees edged one side of the well-stocked garden. Becky and Simon had obviously done well, thought Lucy, as they assessed the large detached Victorian house before them. They had tried ringing the number given to them by Dot, but there had been no reply. With Lucy's resolve slipping again, Jake suggested they call at the house and leave a note, then try phoning again later in the evening. 'They may have gone out for the day.' Lucy had scribbled a garbled message on the page of a notebook begged from the barista in the café and was about to open the gate when a voice behind them said, 'Hello. Can I help you?' Lucy turned to see a young woman, about her own age, approaching with a chocolate brown labrador in tow. She was heavily pregnant.

'Oh, hello. Do you live here? I was delivering a note to Becky Brown.'

'Yes, well no. I'm dog and housesitting for my parents. They're away for another week. Can I help you at all?'

Lucy looked at Jake before explaining for the second time that day, the reason for their visit. The woman listened intently, and her eyes moistened at the mention of Rachel's name.

'This is unbelievable, of course Mum, and Dad, will want to meet you. Oh my goodness, would you like to come in? I'm Hannah, by the way. Oh, and this is Buddy,' she said glancing towards the dog. 'I can take your details and give you Mum's mobile number. She will be so amazed when I tell her.'

Jake had a feeling of déjà vû as they were seated in another unfamiliar sitting room, tea and biscuits proffered, and the bones of Lucy and Rachel's life history shared again.

'Mum always talked about Rachel with such affection,' said Hannah. 'I don't remember her – I was only a baby when she lived with us for a short while – but I know Mum has always felt guilty that she couldn't have done more for her. And she was so concerned about you and how things had turned out for you. She really would be so happy to meet you.' Hannah heaved herself out of the chair she was occupying. 'There's a photo in the hall of the four of them. Hang on, I'll get it.' She returned a minute later and handed Lucy the picture. 'I think it was taken when they lived in London and worked at the bank. Apparently, they used to go clubbing on Friday nights, this is outside Blitz. I think it was *the* place to go back in the day. Look at their outfits, and the big hair!'

Lucy studied the picture. 'I haven't got this one. My Mum, I mean my Grandmother, left me a few photos but not this one. Is that Will? I've got one of him on his own, but I don't know who he is.'

'Oh, didn't you know? He's your father.'

'Oh, I –' Lucy started to reply, trembling with shock, when Hannah's mobile rang. 'Hell's bells! Is that the time? I'm so sorry, I must get this,' she said apologetically, and took the call. 'Oh, right, yes. Sorry, I'll log on now, bye.' She pulled a rueful face, grabbed her laptop from the coffee table and started firing it up. 'I'm so sorry Lucy, I've got a Zoom call. I'd lost all track of time, I'm late.'

'A Zoom call?'

'Yes, it's a sort of video conferencing. I work in IT.' There was a moment's hiatus while no one quite knew what to do next, but Jake could see Hannah was feeling awkward and needed to join this meeting across the internet.

'Don't worry, we've taken up enough of your time. We'll get out of your hair,' said Jake, taking charge. 'Lucy, jot down your mobile number and leave it for Hannah to pass on to Becky. We'll see ourselves out.'

Hannah nodded appreciatively, already introducing herself to other remote conference attendees, and mouthed a 'sorry' to Lucy and Jake as they left.

Chapter 14
1983

'Right, let's have one of all of you now. Okay everyone, say cheese!' Grace clicked the button on her camera. 'One more for luck!' She snapped the assembled group again, before it dissolved into a sun soaked, sand caked gaggle carrying damp towels, buckets and nets back to the hotel. Will brought up the rear, carrying a sleepy Matty, exhausted after a day on the beach.

They had been blessed with an unusually warm few days and Will had been happy to show off Cornwall at its spring time best. Rachel had even commented that it could *almost* have been the Mediterranean. 'At least the sun is shining, and the sea is blue, not that depressing grey we had last time.' Will hoped the weather would hold so as not to dampen her newfound enthusiasm.

It had been strange for Will to visit the tourist hotspots, places where locals rarely went in the season. St Michael's Mount, The Minack Theatre and Lands End had all been on the itinerary and appreciated by Anna and George, but for Will, the happiest times were spent building sandcastles and discovering rockpools with Mikey and Matty on the beach below the hotel. Rachel reluctantly came with them when persuaded, but preferred to lounge in the gardens of the hotel, with a book and a large glass of wine.

Grace and Evie were besotted with their little nephews and came, as often as they could, to help with the rock pooling. They showed the boys how to use nets to catch tiny crabs and minute fish and laughed as they squealed with excitement at the creatures swimming round in their buckets, before being gently released back into their natural habitat. 'We'll make fishermen out of them yet,' said Will.

'Fishy men, what's fishy men?' asked Matty, squinting up at Will and holding tight to his bucket.

'Fishermen, not fishy men. Men who catch fish!' replied Will, laughing.

'I think fishy men is a better description,' said Evie. 'Dan's definitely a fishy man when he comes off the boat!'

'Fishy men, fishy men, fishy men!' chanted Matty, jumping up and down with excitement.

Suddenly, there was a cry from Mikey. 'Look at this daddy!' He was down on his haunches (in the way only little people seem able to do) bending over a rock pool. 'Come here, quick!'

Will climbed over to where Mikey was studiously studying the contents of the pool. 'What is it, Mikey? What've you found?'

'Watch this,' said Mikey, and he prodded a round, browny-maroon, blob, stuck to the side of the pool. The blob opened, and tiny tentacles unfurled. 'Look, look!' he shrieked with glee, as he quickly withdrew his finger.

'That's called a sea anemone, Mikey, and they put out their tentacles to catch their food. He must've thought your finger was his dinner!'

'Well he didn't get me. Look, the tenty things have gone back in.' He prodded the polyp again and the tentacles reappeared.

'Tentacles,' re-iterated Will. 'I think we should leave him now. We don't know if it hurts when we prod him.'

'Can't he go in the bucket?'

'No, he's stuck fast to the rock and it's time to put the other creatures back now, anyway. Come on, time to be getting back to Mummy and Nanny and Grandad.' They gathered up the nets and buckets, and started climbing from the beach.

'Why doesn't Mummy come to the beach with us more?' asked Mikey, as they puffed up the steep path.

'She does sometimes, but she prefers to rest at the hotel,' replied Will, trying to keep the frustration out of his voice.

'That's boring,' said Matty.

'It is a bit, isn't in?' put in Grace. 'It's much more fun on the beach and we love coming with you and Mikey, so tomorrow, how about we go again?'

Will shot Grace a look, but he couldn't be cross because she was right. How could sitting on a sun lounger glugging booze beat getting up close and personal with the tiny natural wonders of marine life found in the pools. He shrugged to himself; he would never understand Rachel.

***

Will had been nervous about his parents meeting Anna and George – they came from such different worlds – and, although they got along at a formal level, he could tell they would never be best buddies. Conversation between the two sets of parents was polite but constrained.

'You do have a lovely view from here Pippa, so different from what we're used to in Camden,' said Anna.

'Yes, we love it and are very fortunate. We wouldn't live anywhere else.'

'We're London born and bred. So much culture to enjoy, do you not miss that down here, so far from everything?'

'No, not really. What can beat this?' she said, as they stood looking across the sparkling sea, white horses riding the tops of the waves. 'And if we want culture, we have a wonderfully unique theatre right on the edge of the cliffs at Porthcurno. Have you been to the Minack?'

'Yes, it's very impressive, but I can't say I'd want to watch a performance sitting on the hard ground at the mercy of the weather.'

'Oh, that just adds to the atmosphere, especially if there's a gale blowing! We all take cushions, rugs, hot water bottles, thermos flasks, it's quite an event!' laughed Pippa. 'And sometimes seals turn up just off the rocks, although they do rather steal the show.'

'Did I hear you say culture?' Seth piped up. 'Ah, we get plenty enough to suit us simple Cornish folk,' he said self-deprecatingly, accentuating his accent and winking at Pippa. 'Now, who's for a drink? George, what can I get you?'

Pippa had cooked up one of her legendary lasagnes and served it with French bread and salad, which they ate on the terrace in a corner of the garden, sheltered by soft pink Tamarisk and vibrant purple Hebe; eleven of them crowded round the table. The usual banter between the Carne youngsters was in full swing, and Anna felt a gnawing envy and guilt that Rachel, her only child, hadn't had the grounding of being part of a larger family. She could see that Rachel found it difficult to join in with the siblings' chatter and felt annoyed with Will at not trying harder to include her. She noticed, with concern, that Rachel was re-filling her wine glass with worrying frequency.

'Will, I think Rachel's had enough to drink,' Anna said quietly, as they helped carry the dirty plates into the kitchen. 'Can you do something? I don't want her embarrassing us in front of your parents.'

Will suddenly had a flashback to his first visit with Rachel and her throwing up in the hydrangeas at the barbeque. He felt a stab of guilt that he hadn't been keeping an eye on her, mixed with anger that he should even have to. He approached Rachel who was now reclining on one of the sun loungers, while everyone around her helped with the clearing up. 'Rach, there are still some dishes to clear,' he said in a loud carrying voice and then, more quietly, 'Can you help? And haven't you had enough booze?'

Rachel flashed him a look and answered in a harsh whisper, 'Oh, well I thought your tight little family unit wouldn't need any help from an outsider like me.'

Will felt his anger building. 'For the love of God,' he hissed, 'what is wrong with you? Perhaps if you even *tried* to join in, you'd be included with open arms. Look, I'm not having this row here, now.

Why don't you go and see to Matty? He probably needs a nap, he's getting fractious,' and with that, Will walked away.

Rachel heaved herself off the lounger and took Matty off to the spare room to put him down for a rest. By the time she returned, Will was getting Mikey ready for a walk. 'Anyone coming to Loe Bar?' he asked.

'I think we should be getting back to the hotel now,' said George. 'It's been so kind of you to have us Pippa, Seth, and good to put names to faces at last. Rachel, are you going with Will or coming back with us?'

'I'd better stay here, Dad, Matty's just gone down for a rest.'

'It's alright Rachel, we'll keep an eye on Matty if you want to go for a walk with Will,' said Pippa, sensing the tense atmosphere between them.

'Oh okay, thanks. Actually Will, d'you mind if I go back with Mum and Dad? I've got a bit of a headache.'

'No, you go. I'll take Mikey for a walk with me.' Will's voice was flat, his expression hard.

'What about you girls, are you going with Will?' Pippa asked the twins, with forced brightness.

'No, sorry. We've got coursework to do,' replied Evie, and Grace groaned.

A kerfuffle followed as goodbyes were said to Anna, George and Rachel; the twins disappeared upstairs to their rooms and Dan swooped through the hall on his way down to the harbour and Uncle Jethro's boat.

'Right, come on Mikey. Looks like it's just us,' said Will, as they prepared to leave.

Pippa caught his arm. 'Are you alright love? What's going on with you and Rachel?'

Will looked down at Mikey, knowing he couldn't have the conversation he wanted to with his mother. 'We're alright Mum, Rach is just tired. See you later,' and he was gone.

***

Will was sitting on the beach, his head resting on his elbows, Mikey propped between his legs humming to himself as he made a pattern out of pieces of driftwood and shells scattered around them. Oh Mikey, Will thought, what are we to do? It seems I can't make your mummy happy, whatever I do. Would she be better off without me? What can I do to change things? Is this all my fault?

'Will? Is that you?' Will looked up to see Tam trudging across the beach, hand shading her eyes from the sun, while her Spaniel, Barney, shot off after seagulls, which he didn't have a hope of catching. 'It is you! Well, fancy seeing you here. Hello Mikey, my goodness you've grown.'

'Tam, what are you doing here? Oh God, did Mum put you up to this?'

'No she most certainly did not and *I* happen to live here. It's as much my beach as yours and Barney needed a walk. I could ask you what you're doing here, city boy!' She crouched down to look at what Mikey had created with the sticks and shells. 'That's a great pattern, you're very clever.' Mikey smiled shyly up at Tam.

'Please don't call me city boy,' said Will. 'I'm not one and never will be. It's the biggest mistake I ever made, going to London. What a bloody mess I've made of my life and I'm only twenty-three. I'm such an idiot.'

'Buddy mess!' giggled Mikey.

Will and Tam looked at one another and couldn't help but laugh at Michael's interpretation.

'What are you going to do? I hate to see you so unhappy.' Tam rested her hand on Will's arm.

'I don't know but something's got to change. When we get back to London I've got to decide; this is killing me.' Will looked down at Mikey who was engrossed in re-arranging the shells and his eyes filled with tears.

'Mikey, do you want to come and help me get Barney? Look, he's right at the other end of the beach chasing the seagulls,' said Tam, sensing that Will needed a minute.

Mikey looked questioningly at Will who nodded his approval and off he went with Tam, holding her hand and chatting away happily.

Thank you, Tam, thought Will, as he fought to pull himself together. Why the hell did I leave you and this place for the so-called bright lights? He wiped his moist eyes and looked out to the distant horizon, feeling momentary peace in this, his thin place. He felt its healing power in his heart.

Tam returned a few minutes later with Mikey on her shoulders and Barney bouncing around at her feet. 'Look Daddy, Barney's got a stick. Throw it, throw it!' he said excitedly. Will duly threw the stick and Barney tore off after it.

'Do you want me to take him?' asked Will. 'He's pretty heavy up there, especially when he's squirming around.'

Tam slipped Mikey off her shoulders and Will hoisted him up on to his. 'Thanks Tam, for giving me a minute, I just ….' but he was unable to say more for fear of breaking down.

'Hey, it's okay. You don't have to explain anything to me. Just take care of yourself and know I'm here if you need me.' They squeezed hands affectionately and trudged back across the beach, Will taking a last lingering look out to the horizon.

***

'Look Rach, it's our last day tomorrow, it's going to be a scorcher, can we at least call a truce for the boys' sake and go to the beach?'

Will and Rachel had had an almighty row, throwing recriminations about like grenades:

'…You said you would lay off the drink and, here you are, sloshed again. It's not a pretty sight, Rachel…'

'…Why can't you pay more attention to me? You're so wrapped up in your cosy little backwater family…'

'…The boys need a mother who isn't half-cut all the time…'

'…And how convenient you got a walk on your own, so you could see that Tamzin…'

'Just stop it! I can't do this anymore Rach,' shouted Will eventually. 'You win. You just carry on poisoning yourself with alcohol, I don't sodding care!' He stormed out of the room, down to the bar and ordered himself a double whisky. How bloody ironic, he thought bitterly, as he drowned his sorrows. By the time he returned to the room, Rachel was asleep on the sofa in their suite, her eyes red from crying. Watching her, Will felt an unexpected tenderness towards her, recognising her vulnerability and insecurity. He lifted her gently on to the bed and, as she stirred, kissed her gently. 'Oh Will,' she said as she responded, and they came together in their desperation and uncertainty for what their future together might hold.

***

'Right, come on boys. Let's see who can catch the biggest crab,' said Rachel, in a concerted effort to enjoy their last day. She was feeling more buoyant after she and Will made up the previous night; maybe the row was what they needed to clear the air, or maybe it was the lovemaking, she thought with a wry smile. 'I'll take Matty over here, you go with Mikey and we'll check what we've caught in five minutes.'

'You're on!' said Will. 'Come on Mikey.'

'You're on!' repeated Mikey.

'On! On!' added Matty, not to be left out.

After a few minutes peering into a deep pool, Mikey suddenly folded over and was sick. 'Daddy, I feel sick,' he said, before vomiting again. Will held him and felt his forehead which was burning hot.

'Rach, Mikey's been sick, and I think he's got a fever,' he called across the rocks. 'I'm going to take him back to the hotel. Are you okay here with Matty?'

'Yes, of course. Do you want me to come?'

'No, stay with Matty. I'll be back soon.'

Will carried Mikey back to their room and stripped off his sicky clothes, sponged him down and gave him some *Calpol*. 'I think you need a rest Mikey, shall I put you to bed?' Mikey nodded, thumb firmly in his mouth and as soon as he was tucked up under a thin sheet, he was asleep. Will found Anna and George sitting on the hotel terrace and asked them to keep an eye on Mikey while he went back to the cove to help Rach carry back the beaching gear.

He scrambled down the path and saw Rachel lying on a towel sunning herself, then saw Matty a little way away on the rocks. But something didn't look right.

'Rach!' he called. He felt a sudden sense of unease and the icy finger of fear gripped his heart.

Rachel seemed to jolt as she sat up. 'What? Oh, hi Will. Where's Matty?' Then she jumped to her feet. 'Oh God, I must've dozed off.' But Will was already scrambling over the rocks towards Matty, lying motionless, face down on the rocks, his head lolling to one side in the shallow water of the rockpool.

'Matty, Matty, oh my God,' he cried, as he scooped up his limp little body. 'What the fuck have you done Rachel? Go and call an ambulance, NOW!'

Rachel stood routed to the spot, tears streaming down her face, unable to move. 'Oh God, no!' she screamed.

'Just bloody GO!' shouted Will, and Rachel started running up the path, stumbling and screaming as she went, with Will coming off the rocks just behind her. As he passed where Rachel had been lying, he glimpsed an empty bottle of Vodka poking out of her beach bag.

Chapter 15

2016

'Hi Lucy, good day?' asked Chloe as they waited at the pool for Daisy and Emily to finish their swimming lesson.

'Yeah, not bad. You?'

'Okay I suppose. Lots of pressure with this blessed Ofsted inspection coming up. Actually Lucy, there's something I wanted to tell you, before Emily tells Daisy, in case she's upset. The thing is, we've decided, at last, to move to Cornwall. You know we've been talking about it for years and we feel, if we don't do it now, we never will. Martin can get a transfer down there and I'll pick up some supply teaching, so we plan to go at the end of the summer term. That way Emily can start at secondary school in Helston in September, and Tom can transfer before he gets too deep into his GCSEs.'

'Oh wow! What a great thing to do, you are brave. Goodness, we'll miss you though.' Lucy felt a sudden stab of sorrow at the thought of her best friend, and Emily's, moving away.

'Look, shall we go for a coffee with the girls and tell them together? Emily's itching to tell Daisy but I said not to, until I'd spoken to you. If they have a meltdown at least they'll do it together with us there.'

As it was, Daisy took the news well and got caught up in Emily's excitement at the prospect of coming to stay in the summer holidays, just as she had this year.

'Seems like they've got it all organised already!' said Chloe.

It wasn't until bedtime that Daisy had a wobble. 'It's not fair, why does Emily have to go? I won't have anyone to go to the girls' grammar with, now.'

'Well, you don't know where you'll be going yet, not until you get the results of the Eleven Plus. But, wherever you end up, you'll be with others from your school. I know it will be hard without Emily for a while, but it looks like we'll be spending plenty of holidays in Cornwall. Starting with half term, remember?'

'Yes, but Ems won't be there then, will she?'

'Well, how about we ask if she'd like to come with us? I'm sure Jake won't mind, but I must check with him first. It might be a bit of a squash in his little cottage, but we'll manage.'

'Yes!' said Daisy with a fist pump. 'Go and ring Jake now!'

'No, I'm speaking to him tomorrow and I need to ask Chloe if Emily can come first, when I see her at school in the morning. Come on, time to settle down now,' and with a kiss and a hug Daisy snuggled happily under her duvet.

***

Lucy was sitting at the dining room table sorting out some activities for the two children she supported at school, a mug of tea in hand, when her phone rang.

'Hello? Is that Lucy? It's Becky Brown here.'

Lucy was thrown for a moment, her head was in school mode, then, like a thunder bolt, it hit her. 'Oh my goodness, Becky. I wasn't sure you'd call. Oh, thanks so much for ringing.'

Becky laughed. 'We only got back a few days ago and it's been manic to be honest, not least because Hannah's had her baby ..... anyway, it's *me* who should be thanking *you*. I couldn't believe it when Hannah told me you'd visited. I .... oh gosh, I'm getting emotional, sorry. It's just that, well, there have been so many times I've wondered what happened to you; so much I want to tell you about your mum. Look, can we meet? We can't do this over the phone.' Becky sniffed loudly.

'Oh my gosh, I'd love to meet you! You're the only person that can tell me about my past. My mum, sorry I mean my grandmother, died a few months ago and .... Oh this is so complicated; you're right, we can't do it over the phone!'

They arranged that Lucy (and Jake, if he could make it) would return to Eastbourne during half term to meet with Becky. Lucy's head was spinning as she came off the phone and she immediately rang Jake.

'I've spoken to Becky, she just rang me! We're going to meet at the end of half term! Can you come too? She sounds lovely and got quite choked up talking to me. Goodness Jake, I can't believe it!'

'That's amazing Lucy, incredible! What a result! You're a super-sleuth! So, do you still want to come down at half term?' Lucy could hear the apprehension in Jake's voice. 'I'd understand if you didn't want to …'

'Of course I want to, try stopping me! I was going to ask; would you mind if we brought Emily with us? Have you got room for another one? It's just that Chloe announced they are moving to Cornwall next year and Daisy was upset, so I suggested Ems comes with us at half term. Is that okay?'

'I don't care who you bring as long as I see you. I miss you so much. I've got bunk beds in the spare room so that'll work. But what about us, you know, sleeping together, will that be a problem? I could sleep on the sofa ….'

Lucy's heart leapt at the thought of sleeping with Jake again, of making love and curling up with him in contentment. 'Hmmm, well it'll happen at some point so may as well be this time. I expect there will be some sniggering on the part of the girls but, hey, it's life!'

'You sound so upbeat Lucy, it's great to hear. Look sweetheart, I've got to go, I'm picking up Mike for rugby practice. Just make any arrangements you need to and count me in! Can't wait to see you and I'll call tomorrow.'

When Lucy finished the call, she was still buzzing, adrenaline coursing through her body. Deep breaths, she told herself, and she started inhaling to the count of four and exhaling to the count of seven. I'll never sleep tonight. The she picked up her phone and dialled Edward.

'Edward, I just had to let you know, I've heard from Becky Brown! We're going to meet her in Eastbourne when we come back from Cornwall in October. How amazing is that?'

'My dear girl, that's marvellous news! Charles, it's Lucy, she's made contact with Becky Brown! Isn't that wonderful? Will you use the flat again, you're most welcome?'

'That would be great if you don't mind. It's a bit of a logistical nightmare to be honest; we're in Cornwall at the start of the week and Emily is coming too, then we're all, including Jake, coming back to drop her off before going on to Eastbourne.' Lucy realised she was jabbering in her excitement, with barely a pause for breath.

'It's good to hear you so cheerful, my dear. I do hope you have a good trip to Cornwall and we may well be at the flat when you're in Eastbourne.'

'That would be lovely Edward. I must get on with some work for school now, but I *had* to let you know. Love to Charles.' Goodness I must've been miserable, thought Lucy, as she ended the call, realising that both Jake and Edward had commented on how cheerful she now sounded.

***

The drive to Cornwall from Kent was, as always, long and tedious but at least Daisy had company and the girls, after their initial chatter, were engrossed in their *Nintendos*, although Lucy made sure they weren't on them for the entire seven hours of their journey to the small hamlet where Jake lived, just along the coast from Poldhu. It had worked out well; Chloe was more than happy for Emily to go with Daisy to Cornwall and, in return, offered to have Daisy when they returned, which meant Lucy and Jake could make their return trip to Eastbourne unencumbered.

Jake's cottage was cosy and quirky, with flagstone floors, low ceilings, steep wooden stairs, an ancient Aga and an even older inglenook fireplace. Despite this, it had a bright fresh look with white painted wood panelling, bright rugs and arty pieces of driftwood. Jake's creations, most of which were abstract coastal pieces, adorned the walls, so the overall effect was of a summer beach house. The girls loved their bedroom, all blue and white stripes, including two squishy bean bags, and bunk beds. After appraising their sleeping quarters and checking out the tiny shower room, they came thumping downstairs. 'Where are you sleeping mum?' asked Daisy.

Lucy gave Jake a look. 'Jake and I are in the double room next to yours.'

Daisy gave Emily a nudge and they both giggled. 'Okay. Can we go in the garden now?' and they tore off to explore the little cottage garden.

'Well, that seemed to go alright,' said Jake, grinning.

Cornwall was blustery but mild, with big seas and squally showers. It was far easier than Lucy thought it would be, keeping the girls occupied. When they weren't on the beach at Poldhu, dodging the waves and splashing around in the stream that flowed to the sea, or drinking hot chocolates from the beach café, they were happily nestled in the bean bags with screens and games. On the day Jake had a shift at the café, Lucy and the girls dropped him off and headed to the Seal Sanctuary at Gweek, reached by travelling along frighteningly narrow lanes and alarmingly steep hills. How does anyone get used to driving here, thought Lucy, as she crept around another blind bend – convinced a vehicle would be hurtling towards her from the other direction – before negotiating a one in five gradient. It was worth the nail-biting journey though, to watch Daisy and Emily exclaim with delight at the recently rescued seal pups swimming about in a pool with the more mature grey seals. As Lucy watched the waters of the Helford River from the sanctuary, ruffled by the wind, she was transported back to the sun-drenched days of summer, kayaking with Jake in this special place.

On their last day, Jake was due to take some paintings to the gallery in Porthleven where they were to be sold. 'It belongs to Tamsin.

She's a jeweller and has had the gallery for years. She sells all sorts of local craft. I'm really pleased, it's the first permanent outlet I've had.'

Tamsin was in the gallery when they arrived. As they piled in to the small space, Lucy gave the girls strict instructions not to touch anything. Daisy raised her eyebrows disdainfully. 'Muuum,' she groaned. Lucy shot her a look and Daisy thought it best not to say anything more.

'Hi Tamsin,' said Jake, giving her a hug. 'I've brought the first load of pictures,' and he put the heavy box on the counter. 'This is Lucy and her daughter Daisy, and her friend Emily.'

'Hello all,' said Tamsin, and gave Lucy a hug. 'It's great to meet you. I've heard all about you from Jake.'

'Oh goodness, not all bad I hope!' replied Lucy, warming at once to the petite woman in front of her, with kind eyes and wild hair only partially contained in a bun. Lucy calculated she must be in her fifties.

'On the contrary, I'd say he's smitten!'

'Please ladies, you're making me blush!' said Jake, laughing.

'Right, shall we get these pictures sorted out? Let's decide where they're going, and Will can help you hang them when he comes in later.'

Lucy sensed Daisy getting restless next to her. 'Look, why don't we leave you to it. I'll take the girls for a wander around the harbour, and we can meet later.' Lucy, Daisy and Emily tramped out of the gallery and ambled along, looking in the other shops and cafes spread along the harbour.

'Can we go out on the pier thing? We went in the summer didn't we Ems?'

'Yeah, but you can only go out there if the orange ball is down, remember? If it's up at the top it means it's too dangerous. Dad got really mad with Tom one year because he went out there and the waves were breaking right over the top. He's such an idiot sometimes.'

Lucy checked and the orange ball was, indeed, hoisted to the top of a sort of flagpole right at the end of the breakwater. 'We'll give that a miss then,' she said, and they retraced their steps and walked around to the other side of the harbour. The tide was out, and fishing boats were lolling on the muddy bottom.

'Look Mum, I think that's the boat we went in last summer. Yes, it is, it's called '*Spirit of the Sea*'.'

'Good memory Daisy, yes you're right.' They looked at the fishing boat, painted bright blue and red with a white wheelhouse, tied up against the harbour wall. A seagull was perched on the bow, like a small figurehead.

'When we went on the boat we caught mackerel Ems, and Jake's friend killed them right in front of us. It was gross!' Then she suddenly shouted to the man on board, 'Hello!'

'Daisy!' said Lucy, as the man turned to see who had called him and she saw it was Mike. Then a woman appeared from the wheelhouse and squinted up at them. Lucy was feeling embarrassed at Daisy's directness. 'Hi, it's Mike isn't it? I'm Jake's friend, Lucy. You took us out on your boat last summer. Sorry, Daisy was excited to see the boat again.'

'Oh yes,' replied Mike, recognition dawning. No one seemed to know what to say next, so Mike continued. 'This is my sister, Morwenna, we've been working on the boat.'

'Hi,' said Morwenna, as she raised her arm in greeting. 'You visiting Jake then? He'll be pleased.'

'Yes, we're down for a few days. He's just dropping off some of his paintings at a gallery, while I entertain the girls.'

'Yeah, Mum said she was taking in some of his pieces. She's kind of adopted Jake as one of her own; he's almost become one of the family. I'm sure his paintings will sell well.'

'Oh, Tamsin's your mum then?' she said to Mike and Morwenna. They gave one another a look and nodded simultaneously. Morwenna said something to Mike that Lucy didn't catch then turned her attention to Daisy and Emily. 'Have you girls seen the grey seal? There's one in the harbour.'

'We saw the ones at the seal sanctuary,' said Emily. 'Is there a real one here?'

Morwenna laughed. 'They're all real, but the one here is living in the wild. Come on, I'm finished here, let's see if he's about.' Morwenna climbed the steep ladder to the harbourside, waved at Mike and led them towards the outer harbour. 'What are your names?' she asked, as they walked along.

'I'm Daisy and this is Emily, but I call her Ems.'

'Ah yes, Daisy. Jake has spoken about you. Good to meet you both, and you Lucy, we've heard a lot about you.' She smiled at Lucy with the same kind eyes as her mother, Tamsin.

'Goodness, I'm surprised my ears haven't been burning, your mum said the same! She's lovely and it's great for Jake to have somewhere to sell his work.'

They continued along the harbour in a companiable silence, Daisy and Emily chattering away ahead of them, until Morwenna called, 'Look, just over there, can you see the head bobbing about?' She pointed a little way out of the harbour and, sure enough, there was the shiny round head of a seal just above the water. It was gone in a flash but, just as the girls started complaining that it had vanished, it appeared again, this time a little closer, as if it had come to say hello especially to them. They watched with delight as the seal seemed to perform in front of them for a few minutes, before disappearing again beneath the waves.

'That was so cool,' said Daisy. 'Will he come back?'

'Oh yes, he's a regular. He often follows the boats as they come and go.'

'Come on you two,' said Lucy. 'Time we were getting back, or Jake will wonder where we've got to. Thanks so much for that Morwenna, it was really special.'

'No problem. I'll walk back with you as far as the gallery.'

Lucy saw that Morwenna was frowning at her as she spoke. 'Everything alright?' She asked.

'Yes, it's just that, silly really, but you look vaguely familiar.'

Suddenly Lucy was jolted back to last summer when Daisy had embarrassed her by saying that she and Mike looked alike, and she asked Morwenna if maybe that could be the familiarity. 'I thought Mike might be my doppelganger,' she laughed, 'but I was more worried that he would think Daisy was being rude!'

They arrived at the gallery and Morwenna offered to watch the girls while Lucy went in to see how Jake was getting on. 'It's a bit tight in there, I'll walk them along to the beach if you like.' Lucy was amazed at this family who seemed so friendly and welcoming; she felt like she'd known Morwenna for years.

As she pushed the door open, Jake was handing a painting to another man to hang on the wall. 'Ah Lucy, you're back, nearly done here.' They finished hanging the artwork. 'This is Will, Tam's husband. Will, meet Lucy.'

Will turned to greet Lucy and she felt a sudden jolt. For an instant they froze, staring at one another. Then the moment was gone. 'Good to meet you at last Lucy. Jake talks about you all the time.' He shook Lucy's hand, looking at her intently with his twinkling brown eyes. Lucy felt strangely moved, unnerved, almost like she wanted to cry, but had no idea why. She gave a wobbly laugh. 'Good to meet you too. Jake, you really need to stop telling everyone about me!'

'Well, why on earth would I do that, lovely Lucy?!'

Chapter 16
1983

Will sat in the dark, the sound of silence pounding in his ears, sleep a distant memory. This had become the norm over the past few weeks. The agonising events he wanted to erase from his memory, played over and over in his mind on some macabre loop: Matty's limp body, Rachel's screams, the ambulance siren, the rattle of the hospital trolley, the swish of the doors, the bleeps of machines. And then the kind voice of the doctor, distorted by the sound of Will's pulse hammering in his ears, telling them that Matty couldn't be saved, that he had drowned.

The following days were a morbid blur. Will couldn't remember much of it, but eventually Rachel had returned to London with Anna and George. He had refused to leave Matty; he couldn't bear the thought of being hundreds of miles away from his tiny body, and while arrangements were made to move him back to the capital for the funeral, he stayed in Cornwall with Mikey. Rachel's only comfort, it seemed, was to be found in the bottom of a bottle, and she could barely look at Mikey – too painful a reminder of Matty, she wept.

Will's family closed ranks around him and Mikey, giving them the love and support they needed to navigate the terrible tragedy. Will walked to Loe Bar daily, the rhythm of his feet pounding the cliff path, temporarily calming his tormented soul. Some days he would scream and roar above the sound of the waves crashing to the shore, beating his chest until it hurt; on others, he would cry like a baby, curled up in a foetal position, wishing the rollers would carry him away. If it wasn't for Mikey, he believed he could have walked into the sea and let it take him. Unbeknown to Will, however, whenever he left the house, one of the family would follow at a discreet distance to make sure he didn't do anything foolish.

Eventually it was decided that Matty should be buried in Cornwall. Rachel was against it, of course, but in her guilt, she was persuaded. Will didn't even care that he threatened her with notifying the police of her drunken neglect of Matty on the beach, to induce her. Matthew George Carne was buried in Porthleven Cemetery, alongside other members of the Carne family who had gone before. It was the saddest day of their lives.

***

A month after the funeral, Will was walking on the beach with Mikey. 'We're going back home tomorrow. It will be nice to go back to Mummy and nursery, won't it?'

'Dunno, s'pose. Can Granny Pippa come too?' Mikey had formed a strong bond with Pippa, and Will knew it would be a wrench for both to be parted. Every fibre in his being screamed at him to stay in Cornwall, but, for Mikey's sake, he knew he had to give it one last go with Rachel. Although he and Rachel had barely spoken, Anna had adopted the role of go-between and convinced Will that she was missing Mikey and wanted to try again. Pippa and Seth were less sure, but promised they would stand by him with whatever decision he made.

'What about Matty?' asked Mikey, looking worriedly at Will. 'Is he coming too?'

Will crouched down to Mikey's level. 'Look out there Mikey,' he said, pointing to the distant horizon. 'Matty's gone to be with the angels, and if you look at where the sea meets the sky, that's where I believe the angels are. Every time we come here, we can feel a little closer to Matty in heaven.'

'Are those fluffy clouds the angels?'

'Yes the clouds can be the angels, they can be whatever you want them to be.' Mikey popped his thumb in his mouth and snuggled into Will.

Tam found them staring out to sea, to Will's thin place, as she approached across the sand with Barney. 'How are you today?' she asked, giving Will a peck on each cheek. She knew a hug would be too much and the tears would start again. She'd found it hard, at first, to comfort Will, not knowing how to be with him, but after the first few weeks he'd sought out her company and they'd slotted back into their special friendship, often walking together along the rugged coast with Barney and Mikey.

'Oh you know, dreading going back. I don't even know if I'm doing the right thing.'

'If you feel you must do it, then it's the right thing, at least to try. You know you can always come home if it doesn't work out.' Tam took Will's hand, hoping in her heart that he would return to this healing place.

***

On his return to London, Will felt like he was being pummelled by a sledgehammer. The constant noise, light pollution, self-absorbed people, traffic chaos. The absence of big skies, dark star-studded nights and salty sea air. Even before he'd done a day back at work, he was longing for the peace of his homeland.

When he arrived home with Mikey, Anna was there to greet them alongside Rachel. Will was shocked at how thin Rachel looked. She flung herself at Mikey, who was taken aback at her overpowering show of affection. They both started to cry, Mikey wriggling to be let go. 'Oh God, I've missed you Mikey,' she said, seemingly unaware of his distress.

'Daddy,' cried Mikey, as he struggled to be released from Rachel.

'Let me take him, Rachel. He's unsure of everything at the moment,' said Will gently, taking Mikey into his arms. Mikey put his thumb in his mouth and nestled into Will's shoulder. Rachel looked at them both, an agonised expression on her face, and walked away.

'Oh God, Anna. How is this ever going to work?' said Will in desperation. 'Maybe I shouldn't have come.' They went into the sitting room and Will noticed that there were no toys anywhere.

'What's she done with all the toys?'

'Oh Will, she couldn't bear to have them here. We've put them all upstairs in Mikey's room. She won't even go into Matty's.'

'Where's my train?' said Mikey, looking around. 'Where's Matty?'

Anna started crying and left the room.

'Hey, little fella. Remember Matty's gone to sleep with the angels, in Cornwall.'

'I want to go to Matty's place with the fluffy clouds. I want Granny Pippa.' Mikey started to cry. So do I, thought Will, as he cuddled Michael. 'Come on, your toys are upstairs, let's go and find them.'

It was hell. Anna stayed, at an attempt to bridge the frozen abyss that lay between Will and Rachel but to little use. When Will returned to work, Anna tried to persuade Rachel to come to nursery with her and Mikey, but she insisted she couldn't bear to be with the other children and dosed up with tranquilisers, leaving Anna to care for him.

Back at the bank, Will was given little time to readjust. A meeting with his boss, a few words of sympathy, and then the expectation that he should be right up to speed with the business of the financial world. When he bumped into Becky in the kitchen, he nearly lost his resolve. 'Don't say anything kind to me, Becky, I won't be able to take it,' he said with a shaky smile.

Becky, not wanting to embarrass or upset Will, kept it practical. 'Okay, I won't but if you need any help at all just let us know. I've seen Rach briefly at home a couple of times; thank goodness Anna is with her.'

'Thanks, appreciate that. God knows what state Rach would be in without her there. It frightens me, to be honest. Look, I'd better go, no rest here for the wicked, or the broken hearted,' he said bitterly.

Becky squeezed his arm as he left with a cup of coffee.

***

Four weeks had passed since Will and Mikey returned from Cornwall. There had been a glimmer of hope for a while after Rachel had been prescribed a new antidepressant medication and was being weaned off sedatives. Her mood lifted, her energy levels increased, and she was starting to re-gain Mikey's trust. She and Anna started taking Mikey to the park together and mixing with other mums and toddlers from playgroup. They were so friendly and encouraging towards Rachel that she was persuaded to come along to the next toddler session. It went well and Anna hoped it wouldn't be long before she could step back and let Rachel resume her life as a mum. Will was encouraged that it might be a turning point, although his heart wasn't really in it. But then Mikey started wetting the bed and having accidents during the day. He'd been dry before the fateful holiday and Rachel couldn't, or wouldn't, understand this backward step. Her only concern was the amount of extra washing.

'Look, why don't you and Mikey go to nursery together today and I'll get the washing done?' said Anna, determined that Rachel should start to take responsibility for her child.

'Anything to have a break from being Mrs Mop, thanks Mum.' Anna was hopeful as Rachel and Mikey set off together; did she imagine it, or was that a slight spring in Rachel's step? She put the washing on then took the opportunity to put her feet up with a cup of coffee, thinking of how good it would be to return to George at the weekend and let Will and Rachel have some time without her, to build their family back together. She had just got comfortable with the Women's Weekly when the phone rang.

'Mrs Askwith, it's Jane from playgroup here. I'm afraid we've had an incident with Rachel; you need to come and collect her and Michael. I'm so sorry.'

When Anna arrived at the nursery, she was shepherded into the office by Jane, the manager. 'What's happened?' Anna said to Rachel, who was sitting on a chair, head bowed, like a naughty schoolgirl waiting for a dressing down in the head teacher's study. She gave

Anna a hard stare and Jane answered. 'I'm sorry Mrs Askwith, but when Rachel and Michael arrived it was obvious that she had been drinking. She was rather unsteady on her feet and some of the other mums commented to me. Then I'm afraid Michael had an accident and Rachel over-reacted; she shouted at him and slapped him across his legs, in front of everyone. We obviously can't have that sort of behaviour from one of our parents.'

'Where's Mikey now? Is he alright? Oh my God Rachel, what were you thinking?'

'Michael is fine. We changed his clothes and he's with the other children having a story.' She didn't add that she'd taken the opportunity to check Mikey for any other signs of abuse. She paused for a moment. 'And I'm afraid we found this in Michael's change of clothes bag.' She held up an empty half bottle of Vodka.

Anna was beside herself with anger, embarrassment and disappointment. They gathered up Mikey, who didn't seem to be any the worse for the morning's upset, and left sheepishly. No one spoke on the walk home and as soon as they were back, Rachel took herself upstairs. When Will returned home later in the day, Anna told him about the incident. He was so disgusted he couldn't even go and have it out with Rachel. 'This isn't working Anna. I can't live like this, and Mikey shouldn't have to, and neither should you.'

'But she's my daughter, Will. I can't just walk away. She needs help.'

'Well, she's not going to accept it from me, is she? And if she won't seek help herself, then I'm not willing to stay here with Mikey. Look at the effect it's having on him. I think the best thing is to take him back home to Cornwall.'

'Oh no, please, that will break her.'

'Anna, she's broken already, and I can't fix her. She didn't seem to give a damn about Mikey today, did she? The booze is always going to come first, just like with Matty.'

'Look, give her another week,' Anna pleaded. 'We'll give her an ultimatum. If she doesn't seek help within the week, you'll go and take Mikey with you.'

Will exhaled deeply. 'If you want Anna, but will it really make any difference?'

Rachel appeared at supper time, dishevelled and contrite. Will could barely look at her.

'I'm so sorry, I don't know what came over me. I just couldn't get past Oddbins. It won't happen again.'

'But it will, won't it? It *always* happens again, doesn't it?' Will could feel his anger building.

'Rachel, this has to stop,' said Anna. 'Will and I have been talking and we need you to promise to seek help within the next week. Go to the doctor, or Alcoholics Anonymous, or do whatever you need to, to get sober. I'll come with you. If it's going to cost money, me and Dad will pay. It's no good for Mikey, you being like this. It's no good for anyone, least of all you.'

'I'm taking Mikey back to Cornwall, Rach, if you don't sort something out in a week. I can't do this anymore,' Will added, giving her a hard look.

Rachel looked from Will to Anna, tears welling in her eyes. Anna and Will stared back at her, Will's heart as cold as stone.

'I promise,' she said. 'I'll call the GP tomorrow.'

'And I'll make sure you do,' said Anna.

***

'Bloody hell, Mikey, you've wet yourself again,' shouted Rachel.

'Rachel, stop it! He can't help it! What d'you expect with what he's been through? It's alright Mikey, come here love.' Mikey stood in the corner weeping.

'What's going on?' said Will as he came through the door, dropped his briefcase and scooped Mikey into his arms.

'Your son's wet himself, again. That's the third time today and the third load of clothes I've had to change, not to mention his sheets from last night.' Rachel stormed off, slamming the kitchen door behind her.

'Rachel!' called Anna. 'I'm sorry, Will. She's been drinking again.' Anna was crying too as she went off after her daughter.

Within an hour, Will had packed bags and gathered Mikey's favourite toys into a box. He bathed Mikey and dressed him in his pyjamas. 'I'm going to pop you into bed now, but when I'm ready I'll lift you into the car and we're going to drive all the way back to Granny Pippa overnight. How does that sound?'

'Will I see Granny Pippa tonight?'

'No, it will be tomorrow morning when we get there, then you'll see her.'

'Is Mummy coming too? And Granny Anna?'

'No, not this time. Mummy isn't very well and Granny Anna is going to look after her.'

'Alright then.' Will tucked Mikey into his bed with his teddy and went downstairs. He felt surprisingly calm, numb almost, as he entered the kitchen. 'That's it. You've had two weeks Rachel. I'm not doing this anymore. Mikey and I are leaving.'

Anna gave a groan and put her head in her hands. Rachel was about to reply but instead leapt up from the table and only just made it to the kitchen sink before vomiting.

Chapter 17
2016

'Here we are again,' said Jake, as they drew up outside the Eastbourne apartment. 'Don't know about you but I'm knackered.' He climbed out of the car and stretched.

'Me too. I don't think driving from Cornwall to Kent to East Sussex in a day is a good move, do you? Ah well, needs must.' They'd taken it in turns with the driving, stopping for breaks at soulless motorway service stations along the way, and delivered Emily and Daisy into Chloe's care in Tunbridge Wells, where they'd had a quick cup of tea, before calling at Lucy's house to collect the photos and letters, then continued on to Eastbourne.

'Ah, here you are!' said Edward, as he welcomed them into the apartment. 'You must be exhausted after that drive. Cup of tea, or something stronger? Charles, they're here!'

Within ten minutes they were raising their glasses of Prosecco in a toast, looking out at a stormy Eastbourne sea. 'Cheers darlings, lovely to see you,' said Charles. 'Now, bring us up to speed with your activities. Did you have a lovely time in Cornwall?'

Lucy entertained with tales of what they'd been up to: walks on the beach; a trip to the seal sanctuary; the girls' delight at Jake's cosy cottage and their giggly reaction to Jake and Lucy sharing a bed. 'But the best thing is that Jake's work is now on sale at the Driftwood Gallery in Porthleven, it's so exciting!'

'Congratulations dear boy,' said Edward. 'It's no more than you deserve. As you know, we loved your paintings when we saw them in the gallery on the Pantiles.' He waved his arm in the direction of the wall on which hung a large seascape of Jake's.

'Thanks, Edward.' Never one for seeking adulation, Jake looked slightly embarrassed, and hoped they hadn't bought the painting just because he was Lucy's boyfriend.

'We *love* it,' gushed Charles. 'Such vibrant blues and purples, topped with brilliant white, just like a tempestuous sea!'

'Ha! They're making you blush Jake,' said Lucy. 'You must start believing in your work, it's fantastic. It must be, or Tamsin wouldn't have wanted it in her gallery.'

'Tamsin? That's a pretty name. It's Cornish, isn't it?' asked Edward.

'Yes, she's the owner of the gallery. She's lovely and so is her husband Will. In fact, Jake knows the whole family; they've sort of adopted him as one of their own. Mike, their son, is the one who took us on the boat last summer. And there's a sister too, Morwenna, who we met this time. Oh, hang on...' Lucy was silent for a minute.

'What?' said Jake.

'No, nothing.' Lucy laughed hesitantly. Suddenly little nuggets of information were popping into her head all at once and she started scrabbling in her bag.

'What is it, Lucy?' asked Edward. 'Are you alright?'

'Yes, no, hang on. Jake, where are the photos?'

'In the overnight bag, why?' Lucy leapt up and a few seconds later, returned with the faded pictures left by Susannah. She spread them on the coffee table and studied them, for the umpteenth time. 'I know this sounds ridiculous, but did you see any likeness between Will and me?'

'What? What on earth are you getting at?' asked Jake, incredulously.

'Bear with me Jake. D'you remember last summer when we first met Mike, and Daisy said we looked alike?' Jake nodded. 'It was so embarrassing,' she added to Edward and Charles, who were both looking more than a little puzzled. 'And his dad is Will, yes?' Jake nodded again. 'Well, when I first saw this photo (she held up the crumpled one of Will on his own) I felt a sort of jolt and then when I met Will in the gallery the other day, I got the same feeling. And this photo of all of them is taken outside Daisy's Cornwall Castle, like that one of Susannah and George in the frame at home.' She turned the picture over and read out the names on the back. 'Look, it says 'Anna, George, Rachel – we know who they are – then, *Will*, Evie, *Michael* and Matty'. You see, Will and Michael, who could be Mike.'

'I don't remember seeing this one before. What are you getting at, Lucy?' said Jake again, taking the photo from her.

'I found it in the back of the safe when I shut it up. It must've slipped out of the pack. I didn't think to show it to you.'

Jake was studying the photo carefully. 'It's hard to say if that's Will, and even harder to see if Michael is Mike. It was taken over thirty years ago. Okay, so we know who Anna, George and Rachel are. Assuming Will and Michael are our Will and Mike in Porthleven, who are Matty and Evie?'

'Do you mind if I take a look?' said Edward. Jake handed him the photo.

'Yes, that's definitely Susannah and George. I wonder why she's called Anna here. Gosh, you do look like Rachel, Lucy.'

'Hang on a minute,' said Jake suddenly. 'Mike has an auntie Evie, one of Will's twin sisters!"

Lucy suddenly stood up. 'Is no one else getting this?' she asked crossly. 'It means that Will, who I happen to have met only yesterday, could be my father!'

***

Later, after a delicious dinner of Moules Marinière with crusty French bread, cooked by Charles, during which they'd ruminated further over Lucy's possible parentage, they watched the news (Edward was obsessed with the view that Brexit would bring nothing but doom and gloom – he was an avid Remainer – and had insisted on watching every news bulletin on the subject, ever since the referendum had resulted in the country heading towards leaving the EU) and then all turned in, feeling wrung out by the evening's events and revelations.

Snuggled up together in the swish guest suite, Lucy said, 'D'you think I'm mad?'

'Possibly, but I love you anyway,' replied Jake, taking Lucy in his arms.

She dug him in the ribs. 'What do we do now? If only I'd made the connection when we were in Cornwall. Now it'll be ages till I can get back.'

'Look, let's see what tomorrow brings, when we meet Becky. She may have some more answers. Then I can talk to Mike and Will when I get back and we can take it from there. It might be better coming from me in the first place. I mean, what if it *isn't* them?'

'I knew it! You do think I'm mad, don't you? You think I'm clutching at straws just because a couple of names have come up in a part of Cornwall that, unbeknown to me, Susannah and George visited, and was then hated by Susannah for the rest of her life.' Lucy sounded petulant.

'No, not at all. There are the photos taken by Daisy's castle, and Evie too, so it *could* be something, but we need to tread carefully. Anyway, we can't do anything just yet and my brain is fried, so can we leave it there for now?'

Lucy harrumphed but didn't argue. She turned to Jake and soon they'd forgotten about everything except each other.

***

The next morning, Lucy and Jake drove to Becky's house; not a day for a walk along the prom as an autumn storm had blown in overnight, bringing rain and strong winds.

'My days, I'm nervous,' said Lucy, as they sheltered in the porch, waiting for the door to be opened. Jake gave Lucy's hand a squeeze but had no time to reply, as the door was flung wide by a tall woman with fair hair scooped up into a clasp, and pale blue eyes adorned with large round tortoise shell glasses. She wore skinny jeans, a loose blouse and ballet pumps. Lucy thought she looked very chic.

'Hello Lucy,' she said in a gentle voice. 'I can't believe we are finally meeting.' She gave Lucy a hug then stood back to study her, her eyes moist. 'You've got Rachel's face with Will's eyes, how lovely. And you must be Jake.' She turned and hugged Jake before inviting them in. Lucy was struck by how self-assured she seemed. Once they were all seated in the lounge, having been greeted by Buddy the labrador, and coffee had been poured, Becky took charge.

'So, where shall we start? Shall I tell you what I can of Rachel's time here in Eastbourne? You can stop me if I'm repeating anything Anna has already told you.' Lucy gave Jake a look and took a deep breath.

'I think I need to explain a few things to you first, Becky,' said Lucy. 'You probably won't believe this, but Anna, whose full name is Susannah by the way, brought me up as her daughter. All my life that's what I was, her daughter. And, no, she told me nothing of Rachel. I grew up believing that Susannah and George were my parents. I only learned the truth after Susannah died last June from a massive stroke.' Lucy saw the disbelief on Becky's face and was on the verge of tears herself. Becky moved to sit beside her, but Lucy held up her hand. 'I'm fine, honestly, let me continue.' She gave Becky a wobbly smile. 'She'd left a letter with my godfather, to be opened in the event of her death. In it, she explained that she was, in fact, my grandmother; that Rachel hadn't been able to keep me and so they, Susannah and George, had decided to bring me up as their own. She gave no further explanation, other than to leave a bundle of photos, letters and birth certificates. She'd kept them locked away in a safe all my life. She said she hoped they would help me and Daisy find my family.' Lucy could feel the bitterness gnawing at her all over again.

'Daisy?' asked Becky.

'Oh, she's my daughter, she's ten and she's amazing. Anyway, the photos didn't help a great deal without any other information, but the letters were the ones you wrote to Susannah when Rachel was here in Eastbourne. They were my only real hope, so Jake and I turned detective and, incredibly, found you.'

'What about George, your grandfather, and Will, your father, couldn't they help?'

'George died when I was one, I can't even remember him, and I only learnt of Will when I saw the photos and we started piecing things together. In fact it was your Hannah who confirmed he was my dad when she showed us the photo you've got of the four of you back in the day.'

'Oh my goodness, this is awful. If only I'd known. I'm so sorry.' Becky dabbed at her eyes with a tissue. 'I always felt bad about what happened, like I should've done more. But Susannah was adamant that we should have no further contact once Rachel had died. I was devastated when we lost her but with a young family of my own, I had to keep going. I was in a bit of a mess myself and didn't want it to affect the family and I suppose life just sort of moved on. That sounds dreadful, I'm so sorry.'

'It's not your fault Becky, and it sounds like you did everything you could to help her. Can you tell me what happened? As you can see, I know very little.'

Becky started at the beginning, when she and Rachel met at the bank and became friends. She told her about Will joining the bank and Rachel's determination to win him. 'She was very strong willed and usually got her way, and such a beauty, the boys were all after her!' Becky smiled at the memories. She continued, telling Lucy and Jake about the heady London scene of the early eighties, of clubbing and drinking, and then of Rachel becoming pregnant. 'I think, if she hadn't been expecting, they would've split up. Will was a gentle soul, not really cut out for the London life and he missed his family in Cornwall dreadfully.'

'Can I ask something?' said Jake. 'Do you know the names of Will's siblings?'

'Gosh, no I don't think so; let me think. No, sorry I can't remember. I know he had a brother and twin sisters though.' Lucy gave a little gasp and grabbed Jake's hand. 'Rachel was a little jealous of them, I think. She was an only child and envied Will's close bond with his family. Why?'

'It's just, we think we may have found Will, but can you carry on and I'll explain later,' replied Lucy.

Becky went on to explain that Michael was born in 1980 and then, seventeen months later, Matty was born. 'I think Rachel decided, if she had one, she may as well have another and get the child-rearing out of the way. That sounds harsh, I'm sorry. But Rachel wasn't particularly maternal, and she was only twenty when Michael was born. Not really ready for motherhood at all.'

'Michael and Matty,' said Lucy in a whisper. 'The two little boys in the photo. And Will with Evie, one of the twins. My goodness Jake, it *is* as we thought.' Lucy retrieved the group photo and showed it to Becky. She studied it closely and her eyes filled with tears. 'Poor Matty,' she whispered, running her fingers over the image.

'Why poor Matty?' asked Lucy. 'Poor both of them I should think, losing their mum when they were so young.'

'Oh God, don't you know?' She looked desperately between Lucy and Jake. 'It was on this holiday that poor Matty drowned.'

'Drowned? Oh no!' cried Lucy.

'I'm so sorry.' Becky was crying now, and Lucy held her, as they wept together for the little life lost. 'It was awful,' she continued at last. 'Rach had been drinking and fell asleep on the beach while Matty toddled off across the rocks and drowned while playing in a rockpool. Will had left Rach in charge of Matty; Michael had been sick and Will had taken him back to the hotel. That's the building behind them in the photo, I think. Apparently, there was a little cove below the hotel and that's where it happened.'

Suddenly Lucy started. 'Oh my gosh, there's a small headstone where the path leads to that beach. Daisy and I noticed it when we were on holiday in the summer – it's got the initials MC on it. Jake, what's Will's surname?'

'Carne. I thought you knew that.'

'No, I've never thought to ask. I was brought up Askwith, and Will's name isn't on my birth certificate, remember. But MC must be Matty Carne. I can't remember the dates on the stone, but we commented on what a short life the child had led. You know, I had a sort of melancholic feeling when we were on that beach and to think, that is where my unknown brother died, I just can't believe it.'

They were quiet for a moment, each digesting the twists and turns of Lucy's life story. After a moment Becky asked if they wanted her to continue. 'Of course, sorry,' said Lucy.

'After little Matty's death everything just fell apart, for all of them really, but particularly for Rachel. Her drinking was becoming a problem before she had the children and we all thought it might improve when she became a mum, but it didn't. If she had a bad day, she'd hit the bottle, but she became very good at hiding it, as alcoholics so often do, and could function quite well, no matter how much she'd had. But losing Matty pushed her over the edge. Will and Anna tried to support her, but she was beyond their help really. When she started rejecting Michael – he was too much of a reminder of Matty – Will left the bank and took him back to Cornwall.'

Lucy was getting unsettled. Where did she fit into Rachel's sorry tale? If Will had returned to Cornwall, how could he be her father? She was beginning to wonder if she'd got it all wrong. Becky picked up on her unease. 'It's okay Lucy, I'm getting to where you come in, but it doesn't make for a happy ever after, as you know. Do you want me to continue, or do you need some time?'

'I was just wondering, if Will had gone back to Cornwall, how can he be my dad?'

'Rachel was already pregnant when he left. She'd confided in me but swore me to secrecy, so when he left, he didn't know.' Becky explained how, eventually, Rachel told Anna and threatened that if she told Will she would terminate the pregnancy. When it was clear that Will had no intention of returning, the house was sold and Rachel moved in with Anna and George to sit out her pregnancy. They'd tried everything to help her get sober, but to no avail. 'We were all amazed that you survived the pregnancy, to be honest, and they did some tests to make sure you hadn't been born with a thing called foetal alcohol syndrome. Thank the Lord you were okay.'

'So what happened to make Susannah and George raise me as their daughter? I still find it unbelievable.'

'Well –,' began Becky, and then Lucy's phone rang. She glanced at the screen. 'I'll have to take this, it's Chloe, sorry.' Lucy answered the call and moved to take it in the hall as Jake explained to Becky who Chloe was.

A moment later Lucy returned, ashen-faced and shaking like a leaf. 'Jake, it's Daisy. She's fallen off the swing in Emily's garden and broken her leg. They're in A&E now.'

Chapter 18

1985

'Happy birthday Mikey,' said Tam. 'Wow, what a great cake. Pippa, did you make it?'

'Yes, Granny Pippa made it. It's Daddy's boat,' said Mikey proudly.

'I can see that, it's such a good likeness.'

'We can blow out the candles now you're here, can't we Daddy?'

'We certainly can. Ready to sing everyone? Right Mikey, ready? One, two, three, blow!' Mikey gave an almighty puff and extinguished all five candles in one, while the family sang Happy Birthday.

***

It was two years since Will and Mikey had returned to Cornwall and it was only now that Will was beginning to heal. It had been easier for Mikey; he was still so young and seemed to have the natural resilience of children. He'd asked after Matty and Rachel at first, of course, but was able to accept that Matty had gone to be with the angels and that Rachel was staying with Granny Anna. As he settled into life in Porthleven, surrounded by Will's loving and caring family, his new life seamlessly replaced his old and now he was happily attending the local primary school.

It took longer for Will. He could hardly bear to think back to the first few months of his return. Days of soul searching, questioning if he had done the right thing and plagued with guilt and self-loathing at what he had allowed to happen to Matty, and Rachel. It didn't matter how many times he was told it wasn't his fault; he still felt dreadfully responsible. Eventually, the inquest into Matty's death was held and a verdict of accidental death given. He was at least thankful that he hadn't gone down the route of incriminating Rachel in the cause of death; it would have served no useful purpose and only added to her distressed state of mind.

He'd tried to keep in touch with Rachel and Anna by phone and letter. Calls had gone unanswered and the only communication he received was a terse letter from Anna notifying him that their house was being sold, that Rachel was living with them, and that they wanted no further contact from Will. He'd replied to inform them of the outcome of the inquest and assured them the door would always be open for contact with Mikey but now, two years on, nothing more had been forthcoming.

While Mikey settled into his new Cornish life, Will continued to feel damaged and adrift. Once again, as in the days immediately after Matty's death, he took the path to Loe Bar, to his thin place, where he could grieve alone; where he needed only the sea and sky to soothe and calm him. He even found himself praying to the place beyond the horizon, for forgiveness and strength to carry on.

Tam was there for him, always supporting but never pushing him, and very slowly he started to mend. They occasionally walked together, further along the coast to Gunwalloe, (he couldn't bring himself to walk the other way from Porthleven, which would eventually take him to the fateful cove where Matty had lost his life) for a pie and a pint at the Halzephron Inn, where they tentatively talked about the future.

'Are you still able to help me with Mikey tomorrow, when we move into the cottage?' asked Will. 'I want him to be there, to be part of it, but not running riot, while Dan and I are humping furniture about the place.'

'Of course. We've got a plan for his bedroom, so you can leave that to us,' she replied cryptically.

'What've you got up your sleeve, Tamsin Trevelyan?' Will laughed. 'Okay, we'll get Mikey's bed in first, then leave you to it.' Will had been lucky to secure the rental of a fisherman's cottage on Mounts

Road and, although it was tempting to stay cocooned in the bosom of his family, he knew he had to move on, to make a life for Mikey and himself.

'You're only moving down the road, Will. Mikey will probably be here almost as much as he is now. And it won't be long before he can walk here on his own.' Pippa had said, reassuringly. But Will knew she would miss Mikey being a permanent fixture in the Carne household.

***

Moving into Sea Spray Cottage (aptly named, given the ferocity of winter storms along this stretch of coast, which often spewed foam and shingle into the streets behind the sea wall) was easier than expected. Will, Dan, Seth and Uncle Jethro worked together to move the larger pieces of furniture into tight spaces within the tiny cottage. As promised, Mikey's room was fitted out first, then he and Tam shut themselves away with a plan of their own. When the bulk of the move was completed, Pippa arrived with a thermos of tea and homemade cakes. Mikey and Tam appeared from the bedroom. 'Come and see what we done to my bedroom,' announced Mikey. 'Come on!' Will and Pippa followed them back up the steep wooden staircase and Tam opened the door with a 'Ta, da!'

Will was almost moved to tears to see how the room had been transformed into a child's marine paradise. Pictures of sea creatures from fish, sea horses and star fish to clams, scallops and oysters, all swimming in a bluey green seascape adorned the walls, painted by Tam and Pippa, with some help from Mikey (mainly red blobs which, he declared with pride, were sea amemomies!). On one wall hung a beautiful painting of Will's fishing boat, *Freedom of the Sea*. 'This is amazing Mikey, aren't you lucky?' said Will. 'How have you managed to paint all these pictures without me knowing?' he added, addressing Pippa and Tam.

'Mainly when you've been working on the boat, haven't we Tam?' said Pippa.

'Yep! And Mikey, you have been so good at not telling Daddy about it, so it was a surprise.'

'And I've got one more thing here for you Mikey,' said Pippa. She popped downstairs and reappeared with a new duvet set sporting a design of cartoon boats and lighthouses.

Mikey was jumping about in his excitement while the cover and pillowcases were put on the bedding. 'I want to get into bed now!' he said, scrambling under the duvet as soon as it was on his bed. 'Night, night!' and he disappeared right under the covers, giggling.

Once Dan, Seth and Jethro had taken their turn in admiring Mikey's bedroom, they all left, giving Will some space to unpack boxes. During the afternoon, Evie and Grace called in with 'Welcome to your New Home' cards and a set of *Lego* bricks for Mikey. He immediately took the set to his bedroom and started building his interpretation of Porthleven harbour.

Later, Seth, Pippa and Tam returned to share fish and chips and a bottle of bubbly with Will and Mikey (without the bubbles) to toast new beginnings. Will felt a surge of love towards them all. Seth and Pippa didn't linger once the fish and chip wrappers were cleared away and Mikey was tucked up in bed, exhausted after his exciting day, and tactfully left Will and Tam alone. They collapsed on the sofa in the little living room with their glasses of bubbly, Will resting his arm across Tam's shoulders. 'Thanks for all your help today, I couldn't have done it without you,' he said. She turned to him and their lips met. Will felt a tiny stab of guilt before the love and desire for the girl he had known since childhood, who had stood by him through the hell of the past few years with no demands or expectations, took over, and they came together.

***

Will and Tam woke early as dawn broke; curtains were yet to be hung at the windows. 'I've wanted this for so long,' whispered Tam. 'To wake up beside you. Are you okay?'

'Do you even need to ask?' replied Will contentedly. 'You are all I want, you always have been, but I was stupid enough not to see it. When I was in London, after Matty died, and it had all gone wrong with Rachel, I was so desperate to be with you, but the guilt was overwhelming, and I was sure you'd find someone else ...'

'Sshh, well I didn't. I'd have waited forever for you Will, you know that don't you?'

'I'm sure I don't deserve you, Tam, but now I've got you there's no getting away.' Suddenly Will gave Tam a tickle and bundled her up in the duvet, pinning her down so there was no escape. She was screeching with laughter and wriggling to get free, when Mikey came toddling into the bedroom. 'I want a go! I want a go!' he shrieked in glee, as he started climbing on the bed.

'Help me Mikey!' laughed Tam, 'he's got me!'

'Aha! Here's another one for my duvet of doom!' Will grabbed Mikey and wrapped him up with Tam and tumbled them about, to delighted peals of laughter, coming from the tangle of duvet.

There was no great declaration that Tam would move in with Will, but over the next few months it seemed to happen naturally; a couple of nights staying over at the weekends, and then, when Will started night fishing, Tam offered to stay with Mikey to relieve Pippa from babysitting responsibilities, until she barely returned home at all. As they settled into a routine built around Will's fishing, Mikey's school runs and Tam's work at the gallery and in her studio, Will continued to heal.

He joined the Carne family fishing fleet and, with a loan from Seth, acquired a share in *Freedom of the Sea*, the boat belonging to Jethro's son, Luke. Dan already worked for Luke, and the brothers worked in harmony with their older cousin. It was a hard existence and Will knew he would never be a rich man, but this was the life he had craved while floundering around in London like a fish out of water. Having spent his early life around fishing boats and the family business, it was in his blood. Being on the sea, at one with the elements, nourished his soul and restored his heart.

***

'Penny for them,' said Tam, as they trudged the coast path to Loe Bar. It was a wild day, too rough for the boats to put to sea, so Will and Tam had a rare opportunity for a walk together, while Mikey was at school. 'You look very pensive, is everything alright?'

'I think so. You know how happy you make me, don't you? And Mikey loves you to bits. And I love our life together. But I still have this awful guilt about Rachel and what became of her; wondering how her life turned out; how much she must hurt not having Mikey with her. Should I have done more to stay in touch, to help her? Will I ever be free of the shame I feel?'

'Do you still love her?' asked Tam tentatively, dreading Will's answer.

'No, that's one thing I'm sure of. I don't think I ever did to be honest, and by the time I realised, it was too late; we were expecting Mikey. Tam, you never need to worry about that.' Will took her face in his hands and kissed her.

'You did what was right for you and Mikey. She rejected you both and continued to do so, even when you tried to keep in touch and offered contact with Mikey. I'm sure if there'd been a change of heart, Anna would have contacted you. And still could. They know where you are.'

'You're right Tam. But will I ever be able to move on with my life completely until I know what happened to Rachel; whether she got well?'

Tam felt a flood of disappointment rush over her – would he ever be free of the spectre of Rachel that lingered between them – and then a rush of compassion towards him, for the burden he continued to carry. 'Only you will know that. You might have to accept that you may never know, or be completely free of it, Will. And I will have to accept that too, which I'm willing to do.' Tam stared up at Will, her gaze full of concern.

'Oh Tam, I'm so sorry. It doesn't diminish what we've got. I love you absolutely and nothing will ever change that. It's just me being a selfish git, trying to ease my guilt, let myself off the hook. Sorry, forgive me?'

'You know you don't have to apologise to me. I haven't been through what you have. I just want to help you get over it, however long it takes.'

'You're a bloody marvel, Tamsin Trevelyan! Come on, I'll stop being a miserable bugger; let's go and blow some cobwebs away, race you across the beach!'

Chapter 19
2016

By the time Lucy and Jake arrived at the hospital in Tunbridge Wells, Daisy was being triaged. After hours of waiting for an X-ray, followed by another lengthy wait for the results, and the fitting of a plaster cast, they finally arrived home in the early evening, exhausted. Chloe had been mortified that Daisy had fallen from the old tree swing in their garden and swore it would be taken down immediately. 'I'm so sorry,' she kept repeating, while they waited in A&E. Eventually, Lucy had persuaded her to go home and pleaded with her to stop feeling guilty. 'It could just as easily have happened to Emily in our garden,' she said, trying to placate Chloe.

Daisy was lying on the sofa with a cup of hot chocolate. 'What did that doctor say about me going back to school? Will I get to stay at home?' she said hopefully.

'He said it depends on the pain. If you're not in pain, you can go.'

'It's not hurting now. Does that mean I'll have to go back on Monday?'

'We'll see. You've been given painkillers so that's probably why it's not hurting now. Let's see how it is when they wear off.'

'This plaster thing feels really weird.' Daisy tapped the cast. 'Can I get it signed at school? Theo did when he had one.'

'I expect so. I'm sure you'll get lots of attention. Now, what film d'you want to watch?'

'I don't. Can I play on my *Nintendo*?' Lucy fetched the device and in no time, Daisy was lost in one of her games.

'I'd better ring Edward and tell him what's happening,' said Lucy to Jake. 'We left all our stuff there. Hopefully they can drop it off on their way back to London. What an abrupt ending to our trip. Such a shame we couldn't finish our talk with Becky. I'll ring her too.'

'While you're doing that, I'll check on train times tomorrow,' said Jake, who was returning to Cornwall the next day.

Later, phone calls made and Daisy in bed, having struggled up the stairs with the cast on her leg (after several attempts at different methods, she sat on the stairs and hoisted herself up on her backside) Jake and Lucy unwound in the living room with glasses of red wine. 'You alright Lucy?' asked Jake, pulling her to him. 'What a day, eh?'

'Honestly, as if we haven't got enough going on, now we've got a ten year old invalid, and, believe me, she's going to milk it for all it's worth!'

'It's you who'll have to cope Lucy, I'm off back to Cornwall. I'd stay for longer but need to get painting again; I want to build up some stock now the gallery has taken a load.'

'You're so sweet to me Jake. Wish we were coming to Cornwall with you but, hey ho, Daisy and I will muddle along, like we always do. Edward and Charles are going to call in on their way back from Eastbourne, mid-week, with our stuff. I couldn't get hold of Becky, she must be out.'

'I'd love you to come. Perhaps you should move down, like Chloe and her family, at the end of the school year. Come and live with me in the land of legends and saints, mermaids and giants.' They laughed together, then suddenly became serious as the idea took hold.

'What?' said Lucy, looking at Jake quizzically.

'Well, why not? You know how much I love you, Lucy Askwith, and we could all squeeze into my little cottage. Daisy would love being close to Emily. And it would save all this driving the length and breadth of the country every few weeks.'

'Oh blimey, I don't know Jake. I'm not sure I could cope with another complication right now.' Lucy gave Jake a kiss.

'Oh, so I'm a complication now, am I?' laughed Jake. 'It's okay, of course it's too much to think about at the moment. I was just getting carried away. So, what's our next step, Detective Inspector Askwith? Am I going to speak to Mike and Will, or do you want to wait until we can do it together?'

'I'd love it if we could talk to them together, but given we're halfway through the school term, the soonest I could come down is Christmas, and I can't wait that long. And, like you said, it might be better coming from you. It'll be a bit of a shock to find they've got an unknown daughter and sister.'

'Leave it with me then, DI Askwith, and I'll report back my findings in due course.'

'Please do DS Robinson and in the meantime, I'll talk to Becky again.'

'Hang on, why are you the DI and I'm only a DS?' laughed Jake.

'I've no idea, but I hope you're not going to disobey your senior officer, or I'll have to reprimand you for insubordination!'

'Blimey, you'll have me in handcuffs in a minute!'

***

Jake returned to Cornwall the following day, thoughts of the night with Lucy playing over in his mind, a contented smile on his face, but he was filled with trepidation about his mission to talk to Mike and Will, though he was determined to help Lucy discover the truth of her past. So here he was, sitting in The Ship Inn, waiting for Mike to arrive. He'd brought copies of Lucy's documents – the photos, birth certificates and letters from Becky to Susannah – in the hope they would help him explain her story. He wanted to speak with Mike first; he was closer to him and knew him better than he did Will.

'Alright Bud?' asked Mike, as he joined Jake with his pint. 'What's all this about then? Your text was a bit cryptic.'

'Alright Mate?' replied Jake. 'Yeah, sorry. It's a bit of a tricky one to be honest, so I'm just going to jump straight in.'

'Right,' said Mike, frowning. 'Go on then.'

'Okay, do you mind me asking about your childhood? I've always believed you were born and bred in Porthleven, is that right?'

Mike's frown deepened. He didn't answer right away, and Jake wondered if he was already treading on sensitive ground. 'Bred, yes, but not born. I was born in London, but Dad and I moved here when I was three. He was born and bred here. Why d'you want to know?'

'D'you remember last summer, when we'd been out on the boat and I met Lucy and Daisy afterwards, and you dropped off my 'phone?'

'Yeah, you'd left it on the boat. Why?'

'Do you remember Daisy saying you looked like Lucy?'

'Yeah, Lucy was really embarrassed if I remember rightly. Where's this going Jake?' Mike was starting to look suspiciously at his friend.

'Look mate, I'm just going to say it, alright?'

'I wish you would, instead of all this poncing about.'

'Right. I think, that is *we*, Lucy and me, think you're her brother.'

'*What?*' asked Mike, astonished. He gave a nervous laugh. 'Is this a joke?'

'Hear me out,' said Jake, and he explained about the death of Lucy's so say mother, Susannah, the letter she'd left explaining that she was, in fact, Lucy's grandmother, and the photos and letters from Becky; how they had started looking into Lucy's past and the tenuous link to Cornwall. 'I've got some photos here; there's one in particular I want you to see.' He handed Mike the photo taken outside Cornwall Castle.

Mike looked at the photo, then up at Jake, and down again at the picture. 'Bloody hell,' he said, 'where did you get this?'

'It was with the papers Lucy's mother, well grandmother, Susannah, left. So, are you the Mikey in that picture? And is that Will and Evie? That's what it says on the back.'

Mike studied the photo again, then looked at the caption overleaf. He gave a massive sigh, shaking his head in disbelief. 'Yeah, that's us. Another lifetime. I can't get my head round it. Rachel, in the photo, is my mother, and Anna and George are my grandparents. I've never seen any of them again, since we moved down here when I was three.' He told Jake about the holiday in Cornwall, how Matty, his younger brother, had drowned. 'I can't really remember much about it, only what I've been told, but afterwards Mum and Dad fell apart and split up. I believe Mum had mental health problems and I know she was a drinker. Apparently, she couldn't cope with me, so dad brought me down here. To be honest, no one ever talked about it and it became 'the big family secret'.' Mike wiggled his fingers, indicating quote marks.

'I'm sorry to hear that, Mate.' Jake handed Mike the first two letters from Becky, telling of Rachel's time in Eastbourne. 'Becky was one of Rachel's closest friends and we managed to track her down. We met her just the other day and she confirmed everything I've told you.'

'But how does that make Lucy my sister? I don't see how she can be if Mum and Dad split up soon after the accident.'

'Apparently, Rachel was pregnant when you and Will left, but she didn't want him to know and swore your grandmother and Becky to secrecy. I believe she threatened to terminate the pregnancy if Will was told.'

'Bloody hell. Sounds like she was pretty screwed up, doesn't it, my mother? In fact, it sounds like the whole family was. I mean, why would my grandmother change her name from Anna to Susannah and then bring up Lucy as her daughter? Poor Lucy, what a shock to find this out.'

'Yeah, and for Susannah to tell her by letter after her death. According to Lucy, she suffered badly with her mental health all her life, which is hardly surprising knowing what we do.'

'I wonder what happened to Rachel. Is she still in Eastbourne?'

Jake handed Mike the last of Becky's letters. 'She died, Mike, I'm so sorry mate. It says so in the letter. We haven't spoken to Becky about it yet,' and he explained about their visit being cut short by Daisy's accident.

***

Mike decided he would talk to Will alone about what he had learnt from Jake so, the next day, he walked with his father to Loe Bar. It was one of those exceptional autumn days, when the sun shone and the temperate Cornish climate, influenced by its proximity to the Gulf Stream, brought mild maritime air and temperatures soared into the high teens. They stood together on the sands, shielding their eyes from the low autumn sun, watching seabirds wheeling languidly in the sky above them.

'It's a while since we've been here together, to our thin place, just thee and me, isn't it?' said Will. 'Does it still calm you as much as it does me?'

'It brings me peace, Dad, like nowhere else. That's why I wanted to bring you here, because I've got something big to tell you and we've always had our big discussions here, haven't we?'

'We certainly have. So, what is it Mikey?' It was a long time since Will had used Mike's childhood name.

Mike explained, as clearly as he could, everything Jake had told him about Lucy's search for the truth about her life and how, incredibly, it had led to Porthleven. When he showed Will the photo taken outside Cornwall Castle, Will wept as he gently touched the image of little Matty. '... and so we know Rachel died in Eastbourne, but Lucy is hoping Becky may be able to tell her more about the circumstances and why Anna let Lucy believe she was her mother.'

Will and Mike stood in silence, looking towards the horizon, each lost in his own thoughts. Eventually Will spoke. 'I want to go and see Becky. She was good to us in London, and she always looked out for Rachel. I'd like to hear for myself how it was, lay a few ghosts and understand more about Lucy's childhood. Poor girl, what a start she must've had in life.' Mike put his arm across his father's shoulders.

'Good grief dad,' Mike said gently, 'I've got another sister and you've got another daughter. What will Tam and Wenna think?'

'Only one way to find out; we must tell them straight away.' They left the beach and made their way back to Will and Tam's house set high above the village. It was the usual Saturday routine in the Carne household. Morwenna, who still lived at home with her parents, was looking after Mike's four-year-old, Ross, while Mike's wife, Sarah, took Freddie swimming. Tam was in her studio, attached to the house, working on her latest jewellery designs. Will gathered Tam and Morwenna into the kitchen, while Mike settled Ross in front of his favourite DVD, *Finding Dory*, then joined them.

'Righto,' said Will, when everyone was settled, 'I need to tell you something so unlikely that you probably won't believe it but hear me out.' He wasted no time in relating Lucy's story, which sounded even more fanciful as he told it himself, punctuated by remarks from Mike where he thought Will had forgotten an important point, or something needed further explanation.

'I can't believe it!' said Tam. 'Jake's Lucy is your daughter? It's impossible. How could that be? Oh Will, Mike...' Her eyes were moist, and she gave them both a hug.

Morwenna watched the exchange, then said, 'I thought there was something about Lucy when I met her, some sort of connection. Hey, I've got a big sister!'

'Yeah, and I've now got two younger sisters. What bad luck is that?'

'Daaad,' came a call from Ross in the sitting room. Mike and Morwenna went off together to see to him, still teasing one another about who had the better deal in having an additional sibling.

'Lucy's your daughter. I just can't get my head around it,' said Tam, as she stood in Will's embrace. 'That poor girl, sounds like she had a raw deal, growing up. Fancy Rachel rejecting her and then her grandmother pretending to be her mother. What makes someone do that? And not telling you, Will, that you had a daughter; how cruel. We *must* welcome Lucy and Daisy into the family Will, after all, we are all she's got now.'

Will felt huge relief and a surge of love for Tamsin; so typical of her generous nature to accept another aspect of Will's past with grace and understanding. He squeezed her tight. 'How can I be lucky enough to have someone like you?'

***

'So how did it go?' asked Lucy, when Jake rang for their usual evening catch up. She was on edge, wondering how the Carne's would have taken the news that Lucy was part of their family. She wasn't sure she could cope with the rejection if they didn't want to know.

'Pretty amazingly, actually,' said Jake, a sense of pride in his voice. 'Must be that empathetic touch I've got! Seriously Lucy, they want to welcome you with open arms, but also Will wants to meet with Becky himself, to hear first-hand what happened to Rachel. She was a good friend to him back in the day and as she helped Rachel so much, he feels he owes it to her to thank her for trying.'

'Oh my days, Jake, that's such a relief. I was having nightmares of them all telling me to push off; that they didn't want me in their lives. I can't believe it.' Lucy eyes glistened with unshed tears, the sudden release of the pent-up anxiety flooding through her.

'Well, sweetheart, they do want you in their lives so there's no worries there. Did you speak to Becky?'

'Yes I did, but she's been up to her neck with her own family. Hannah's baby got rushed into hospital the day after we visited with a really high temperature, so she's been supporting her. She said she'd be in touch when things had calmed down.'

'It all seems to be happening, doesn't it? Well, maybe we can arrange to meet with Becky together – Will, Mike, you and me – what d'you think?'

Lucy felt her stomach tie itself in knots. 'Yeah, maybe, but don't you think I should meet my dad and brother properly first? And there's Daisy to consider too, of course. And what about Tamsin and Morwenna? Oh my life, this is so complicated.'

It had taken some organising, but after lengthy phone calls between Kent, East Sussex and Cornwall, and intricate diary scheduling, a plan was hatched for the beginning of the Christmas holidays. They had tried to arrange the meeting during the second half of term, but Lucy was tied up with the festive chaos of school nativity plays and carol services, so it was agreed to wait until it was over.

Lucy had kept Edward up to speed with developments and he and Charles insisted that they stay at the Eastbourne flat when they visited Becky again. 'Oh my, it's so exciting for you!' Edward enthused. 'How marvellous it will be to meet your father and brother; we couldn't be happier for you that it's all worked out so well.'

Chapter 20

2016

'Daisy, have you finished packing?' Lucy called up the stairs. 'They'll be here soon.'

Daisy came clumping down, her leg now in a supportive boot rather than a plaster. 'Yes, I've packed. I still don't see why I couldn't of gone Christmas shopping with Ems; there's loads of time,' she said grumpily.

'Couldn't *have*,' corrected Lucy, automatically. 'You know why not: Jake, Will and Mike are coming today, and we need to have everything ready for going to Eastbourne tomorrow and then down to Cornwall for Christmas.'

As soon as the school term had ended, carol service and nativity play duly accomplished for another year, Lucy had gently explained to Daisy their connection to the Carne family, in as simple terms as possible. Typically, Daisy had taken it in her stride – 'I *told* you Mike looked like you! See, I was right!' – and was excited by the fact that she had suddenly acquired several cousins, and a large extended family with access to a fleet of fishing boats. She wasn't so sure she'd enjoy the coming few days, meeting her grandfather and uncle Mike again, then travelling to Eastbourne to see Edward and Charles, when she'd rather be doing the usual Christmassy stuff at home and seeing plenty of Emily. Things started to look up, however, when she learned that Edward and Charles would be taking her to the pantomime in Eastbourne while the 'grown-ups' visited Becky.

Lucy was on edge all day waiting for Jake, Will and Mike to arrive. She'd prepared a large pot of beef bourguignon, which was simmering away in the slow cooker, and had packed the car ready for their road trip. She was just putting the last few Christmas presents in the boot when they arrived. Her heart was racing as she watched the men disembark from the car. Jake was the first to greet her with a big hug and a kiss. 'Alright sweetheart? It's so good to see you.' He could see how nervous Lucy was. 'It'll be fine, don't worry.'

Will and Mike made their way over to Lucy, and Will held his arms open for a hug. His eyes were moist as he let her go. 'Lucy, it's so good to meet you again. My daughter, oh my goodness. I'm so glad you found us, it's such a privilege to welcome you into our family.' Lucy found it so natural to be embraced by her father and a warm sense of comfort and relief flowed through her, the uncertainty of the last few weeks melting away. She wiped her eyes.

'It's good to see you again Lucy,' said Mike, with a grin on his face. You realise my life is going to be hell now, with two younger sisters. Morwenna thinks it's great she's got an ally and can't wait to tell you all my secrets!' He too opened his arms and Lucy went in for a hug, laughing happily, her anxiety melting away.

Jake noticed Daisy standing shyly by the door and went over to her. 'Hi Daisy, how's the leg? I see you've got a boot now, must be better than the cast.'

'Yes, it is. I've still got my cast though, the doctor cut it off and let me have it because it's covered with signatures. You can sign it if you like.'

'I'd love to. I'll have a look at it later. D'you want to come and say hello to Will and Mike?' Daisy gave Jake a worried look and put her hand in his. 'It'll be okay, don't worry,' he whispered comfortingly.

Will and Mike greeted Daisy without over playing it; they didn't rush in for a hug or even a handshake but were led by her. She studied each of them in turn, her hand still firmly in Jake's. 'I was right, wasn't I? You and Mummy do look alike,' she said to Mike.

'You certainly were – good powers of observation there,' replied Mike.

Then she turned to Will. 'I don't really know what to call you. I'm a bit confused at the moment because my granny turned out to be my great granny and now I've got a new grandad and a step granny.'

'That *is* confusing. You can call me Will, if you like. Whatever you're happy with. Or I could be Granfer.'

'Granfer? What's that?' replied Daisy, frowning.

'It's a word we use for grandfather in Cornwall.' Will's eyes twinkled as he studied Daisy's serious face.

She thought for a moment, then her face cleared. 'What if I call you Grandad Will? My best friend Emily calls her granny Grandma Sue, so she doesn't get confused with her other granny.'

'That sounds good to me.' Will smiled kindly at his granddaughter.

'Well, I'm glad that's settled,' said Lucy. 'Shall we go in? It's freezing out here.'

***

The drive to Eastbourne was slow, the roads busy. 'I don't miss this traffic,' said Jake. 'It's so quiet in Cornwall now we're out of season, but it never dies down in the south east, does it?' They'd travelled in Will's car from Porthleven, Mike and Will sharing the driving, and now Lucy and Jake were in her car with Daisy, while Mike and Will followed in theirs. 'I think it went really well yesterday, what about you?'

'It went better than I ever dreamed it would,' replied Lucy, with a lightness in her voice. 'I feel like I've come home, if that makes sense. It's like there's always been a missing link and now there isn't. Does it sound corny to say I feel complete?' She glanced at Jake, suddenly feeling embarrassed.

'No of course not. You've had such an isolated life, having to be so self-sufficient and responsible from such a young age; it's high time you had the chance to be nurtured, with a wholesome and loving family around you. Oh, and a partner who is completely devoted to you.' Lucy squeezed Jake's hand and glanced in the rear-view mirror to see if Daisy had overheard their conversation, but she was engrossed in *Super Mario* on her *Nintendo Switch*.

They travelled on in contented silence, Lucy re-playing the conversations from the previous evening when she and Will had shared their life stories. Lucy recognised that her mother and father were never really suited. They had come from totally different backgrounds, and had Rachel not been pregnant with Mike, they were unlikely to have stayed together. It seemed to Lucy that Will still carried the guilt of how his life had gone so tragically wrong at such a young age. It made her realise that she made the right decision, all those years ago, when she found she was expecting Daisy, not to stay with Danny just because he was the father of her child.

Lucy was blown away by Will's reaction to her own story, his compassion for her growing up, as she did, in the unstable orbit of Susannah's unpredictable mental health; his sadness that he had been unaware of her existence and his promise that he would make up for the lost years without her.

'Right, here we are,' said Lucy, as they drew up at Edward and Charles' apartment block. 'And we didn't lose Will and Mike along the way.'

Edward and Charles were, as ever, the perfect hosts, offering their own unique brand of hospitality: coffee and delicate pastries on arrival (with a frothy milk shake for Daisy, which she drank while swinging in the Egg chair looking over the bay – 'this is *so* cool'), followed by a walk to a swanky restaurant in the Sovereign Harbour for a slap-up meal (insisting they foot the bill). Lucy watched Mike's reaction to the couple with amusement; this was outside his normal area of experience – fishing boats, Saturday rugby and a pint at The Ship Inn – but he lapped up their easy flamboyance and bonhomie and loved that they were as intrigued by him as he was by them. Once they knew he was a chef at one of Porthleven's local fish restaurants, they were immediately planning a visit. 'My dear boy, we simply *must* come and sample your menu, especially as the fish will be straight off your very own boat. How exquisite!' gushed Charles. At the mention of them going to Porthleven, Daisy piped up, 'You'll love it there and you might see the seal we saw at half term. It was swimming in the harbour.'

After lunch, Edward and Charles took Daisy off to the theatre to see Cinderella, while Lucy, Jake, Will and Mike made their way to Westleigh Avenue and The Firs. Suddenly, Lucy's disposition changed, and the lunchtime frivolity was replaced with uncertainty, as they delved back into the past again. 'Are you feeling how I'm feeling?' asked Will, picking up on her mood. 'I'm rather nervous to be honest. It will be good to see Becky and Simon again after so many years, but difficult to hear about Rachel.'

With that, they arrived at the house and, after greetings and introductions, were ushered into the sitting room. Lucy had worried it might be awkward between Will, Becky and Simon, but everyone seemed relieved to have finally met and to have the chance to lay some ghosts. Once they'd dispensed with the 'you haven't changed a bit', 'good to meet you Mike, the last time I saw you was …' comments, Becky started things off. 'So, I expect Lucy has told you what we talked about when she visited a few weeks ago, but I know you all want to understand how it came about that Rach ended up here and why Anna/Susannah, brought you up as her own daughter, Lucy.'

'Yes we do,' said Will, and Lucy nodded beside him.

'Well, as I told you before, Rach moved back home with Anna and George while she was pregnant and then you, Lucy, were born. We were all hoping, because you were a girl, she would be able to accept you, after poor Matty's death and her struggle to look after you, Mike, but, I'm so sorry Lucy, she went back to the drink. I visited regularly – Anna said I was the only person Rach would listen to – but it didn't make any difference. She couldn't cope and Anna was more of a mum to you than Rach could ever be. Then one day, Rach just walked out. She went on a bender, and we didn't know where she was for days. Anna was too scared to go to the police, in case social services became involved and took you into care. Anyway, eventually Rach turned up here in Eastbourne. She was in a terrible state, so we took her in. She made me swear not to contact Anna and for a while, I did as she asked. But in the end, I had to contact her. We couldn't go on supporting Rach and I had Hannah by then. I went to see Anna myself. I turned up literally as a removal van was packing up their belongings. They were moving away with you. If I'd come a day later, I'd have missed them.'

'What? They were just taking me away, without telling Rach?' said Lucy, her voice trembling.

'Well, yes. All Anna said to me was that Rach didn't deserve the chance to be a mother again and that they were taking you somewhere new, to give you a better life. She didn't want Rach to know where they were going.'

'So Susannah just decided to take me and bring me up as her daughter, without involving Rachel? Unbelievable!'

'I suppose she thought it was the best way. I pleaded with her to let me keep in touch, now that Rach was with us, and we agreed I could write to her, and she would send money to support her. I wasn't to let Rach know they had moved and nor was I to let her have the money – she didn't want her to spend it on drink – but I could use it to help her. She was so determined that I shouldn't know where they were going that she set up a PO box number for our correspondence.'

'What a responsibility to put on you,' said Will. 'I'm so sorry Becky.' Becky smiled weakly at Will. Simon, Becky's husband, came and sat beside Becky and took her hand. 'She's a strong person, is Becks, and a brilliant one. Always has been, always will be.'

Becky gave him a friendly nudge and continued. 'So, we agreed I would write every six months to let her know how Rach was doing. At first, things were better – she started going to Alcoholics Anonymous and was put on a programme to get her off the booze. We found her a little bedsit, which Anna's money paid for, and Rach got a job in a typing pool. We were hopeful, for a while, but then at Christmas she fell off the wagon again.'

'Par for the course,' mumbled Will to himself.

Becky looked sympathetically at Will. 'After that, she just spiralled. Then, one day she decided she wanted to go to London to visit Anna and George, and see you, Lucy. We tried to persuade her not to go but she was adamant, so I had to tell her they'd moved. She went crazy – furious that they had moved, had taken her daughter away, that I knew and hadn't told her – it was awful.' Becky paused and wiped a tear from her eye. 'She stormed off and we didn't see her alive again. After a few days, when I hadn't heard from her, I called round at the flat and found her.'

'Oh Becky, no!' exclaimed Lucy. 'How awful for you, I thought the police found her.'

'No, it was me. Obviously, the police were involved afterwards, and I told Anna it was the police, it just sounded less personal somehow. She died of an overdose of sleeping pills and booze. I wrote one more letter to Anna to tell her and then said I wouldn't be in touch again. I just couldn't. I can't believe she didn't tell you, Will. If only I'd known.'

'It's not your fault Becky.'

'So, yes, I think, when they moved from London, she decided to bring you up as her own daughter, Lucy; she'd been the one who had raised you from birth and I suppose she couldn't bear the thought of Rach claiming you, which is why she didn't want me to know where you were, in case Rach found out. Maybe that's why she reverted to her full name, Susannah, to distance herself further from the past.'

'It's all so sad,' said Lucy. 'And had a devastating effect on her, even though she must've believed she was doing the right thing. Then when Rachel died, and George too, she was left carrying the secret alone. No wonder she became ill.'

'And you had to deal with it, as a child Lucy. It's wrong on so many levels and I'm so sorry,' said Will, stroking her back.

'I think we all have things we're sorry about, things we wish we'd done differently,' said Simon, 'but I don't think any of us could have saved Rachel from herself. I hope, though, we will find today has been cathartic and we can finally lay Rachel's ghost to rest.'

'Yes, you're right Simon,' agreed Will. 'It has certainly brought a further level of closure and, thanks to the letters you sent to Anna/Susannah all those years ago, Becky, Lucy has found her family, for which I will be eternally grateful.'

'Me too,' agreed Lucy.

'And, can I just say, it was my experience with Rachel that led me to becoming a social worker, a career I have loved for over thirty years, so I have to credit her with that,' added Becky.

'And a bloody good social worker she is too,' said Simon. 'Now, who's for a cup of tea?'

***

After meeting with Becky and Simon and learning the sad story of Rachel's final few months, Will, Mike, Jake, Lucy and Daisy spent another night with Edward and Charles, Daisy giving them a blow-by-blow account of the pantomime over a pre-Christmas meal, and then travelled on to Cornwall for the festive season.

Will and Lucy spent time together, just the two of them, learning of each other's lives and getting to know one another. They walked the coast path to the cove where Matty had died, and Lucy was transported back to last summer – was it only five months ago? So much had happened in that time – when she and Daisy had come across the cove. 'How often do you come here?' she asked Will.

'I couldn't bring myself to, for years after the accident, but eventually Mike and Tam persuaded me to come and make my peace with the place and we put the headstone there in memory of Matty.' They walked over to the small granite stone and lay their hands on it before climbing to the beach. 'It was over there on the rocks,' said Will, pointing to an outcrop. Lucy remembered the feeling of melancholy she'd experienced as she stood there on those very rocks back in the summer.

'Oh gosh, that's where Daisy clambered last year,' Lucy replied, and shivered at the memory. 'I'm so sorry.'

They stood together for a moment, Will's arm protectively across Lucy's shoulders, before climbing from the beach and starting the trek back. Lucy told Will of her childhood with Susannah, her escape to university and the devastation of finding herself pregnant. Will's eyes filled with tears for his eldest daughter, but Lucy was not one for pity. 'Daisy was the best thing that happened to me. It was difficult, but I wouldn't change a thing.'

'You're a strong woman, Lucy,' said Will. 'You are very like Tam in many ways.'

'I'll take that as a compliment, she's a lovely woman, one I'm now lucky enough to call my step-mum!'

Will exuded love for Tamsin and explained how difficult it had been to move to London, to further his career on the advice of his father, leaving her behind. 'I didn't realise, until it was too late, just how much I loved Tam, and I was so lucky that I didn't lose her. She's been through a lot with me. I was a wreck after Matty died but she was always there, never demanding anything from me or expecting more than friendship. Of course, we got together in the end, but I could never make the full commitment because of the guilt I felt about Rachel. Even though Rach and I were never married, I didn't feel I could marry Tam.'

'And now? Now you've laid Rachel's ghost to rest?'

'Well yes, if she'll have me, it's high time I made an honest woman of her, and you're the first to know that I'm going to ask Tam to marry me, and very soon!'

Christmas had been a revelation to Lucy, spent with Jake and her newly acquired extended family. There seemed to be a countless number of Carne's – aunts, uncles, cousins first, second and removed – so in the end, she and Daisy, with help from Mike and Morwenna, drew a family tree to make sense of who was who. Lucy was amazed when she met her grandparents, Pippa and Seth (she'd had no idea they were alive and well and living in Porthleven), and Daisy was delighted to have not only new grandparents, but also great grand-parents. Lucy was nervous at first, not sure if she would be accepted or fit in with the gregarious relatives, but they were all so warm and welcoming it was as if she'd known them forever. Daisy was rather overwhelmed to start with but, once she realised she was the eldest of the cousins and second cousins, and had a following of devoted little ones, she clucked around like a mother hen with a brood of chicks.

After the raucous festive celebrations at Will and Tamsin's, which included a marriage proposal with copious amounts of champagne, it was a pleasure to return to the peace of Jake's cottage and snuggle up by the wood burner, to watch traditional Christmas movies.

'I love your cottage,' Daisy ventured one evening, before climbing the narrow stairs to her tiny bedroom. 'It's like my Wendy house only bigger. But not as big as a real house.'

Lucy and Jake laughed. 'It is a real house, Daisy, just a small one,' said Lucy.

'I know that,' Daisy replied, raising her eyes to the ceiling. 'I was *joking*!'

Lucy and Jake gave each other a look. 'Right, off to bed now young lady, and don't forget to clean your teeth,' said Lucy. With another raise of her eyes heavenwards, Daisy scuttled off up the stairs.

'This has to have been the best Christmas ever,' said Lucy, as she cuddled up to Jake. 'I'm going to miss everyone so much when we go back. I can hardly bear it.'

'Well, my suggestion still stands. Move down here at the end of the school year. You'd be with me, nearer your family, and Daisy would be able to keep her best friend. What's not to like?'

Lucy was quiet for a moment, then turned to Jake. 'You know what, why not? There's nothing keeping me in Kent now, and it's the perfect time for Daisy as she'll be changing schools anyway. The thing is, I'd have to find somewhere to live.' She gave Jake a knowing look, a playful smile on her lips.

'Don't be daft, you can move in here. You heard Daisy say how much she loves my little Wendy house and it's just about big enough for the three of us.'

'Is that an official invitation then, Jake Robinson?'

'I rather think it is, Lucy Askwith! What do you say?'

'I say YES!'

Epilogue

2017

Lucy and Daisy shut the door of the Wendy house in the garden for the last time. 'Are you going to miss it?' asked Lucy.

'A bit, I suppose,' replied Daisy, 'but I'm getting too big for it now, and it's not really cool is it, at my age?'

'No, I suppose not, at your great age,' laughed Lucy. 'Come on then, let's get on the road. We've got a long drive ahead.'

They walked over to the house, hand in hand, but didn't go inside again. Once the removal men had finished loading up the van and they'd cleaned each room behind them, the empty echoing spaces had upset Daisy, so they'd put the last of their belongings in the car and locked the door. End of an era, thought Lucy, as she blinked back tears.

***

Lucy and Jake stared out to the horizon, sitting together on the beach at Poldhu Cove. Daisy was at a sleepover with Emily, the first get together since they'd all made the move to Cornwall, and after Jake finished his shift at the beach café, he and Lucy had taken a picnic on to the sands to make the most of a perfect summer evening. The crowds who had flocked to the beach for the day were leaving in dribs and drabs, returning the cove to its natural tranquillity.

'Have you heard of thin places?' Jake asked Lucy, as he handed her a chilled glass of white wine from the cool box.

'No, what's that?' replied Lucy, squinting at Jake before pulling her sunglasses down over her eyes.

'Well, they say it's where the veil between this world and the next is supposed to be thinner, where people feel closer to the spirit world, or heaven, or God, or whatever is their thing. That is, if you believe any of it exists.'

'And do you?'

'Yes, I think I do. When Mike and I got talking about his past, about Matty's death, he told me of his and Will's thin place, the beach at Loe Bar. They went there regularly when he was a boy and they both felt a closer connection to Matty there. And they still go to this day.'

'So can it be anywhere you want it to be then?'

'I believe so. Often they're on the coast, where land meets sea, or sea meets sky on the horizon. And according to legend, Celtic saints often referred to 'thin places'. There's supposedly one at Cape Cornwall over in the west of the county, where St Piran, Cornwall's patron saint, is said to have landed from Ireland in the 5th Century, but people have their own thin places, wherever they feel it I guess.'

'It's a lovely idea.' Lucy lifted her eyes to the distant horizon and allowed her mind to drift. 'Perhaps this is my thin place,' she said dreamily, as a great sense of calm settled upon her.

'I find it comforting, relaxing, restorative. Except when there's a storm blowing of course! But even then, the majesty of it stirs the soul and lifts the spirits.' Jake put his arm across Lucy's shoulder. 'Goodness, listen to me waxing lyrical!'

'I love it. There aren't many blokes so in touch with their spiritual side.'

'When I first came down here, licking my wounds after splitting up with my ex, I walked for hours on the beaches and along the coast path trying to make sense of everything. Eventually, just sitting here on the rocks and communing with the place beyond the horizon gave me the peace I craved. I didn't think of it as a thin place until my conversation with Mike, but now I realise that's what it is.'

They continued to stare out to sea as the sun sunk lower in the sky. Then Jake took Lucy's face in his hands and gently turned her towards him. 'Lucy, I would love to share the rest of my life with you, and Daisy of course, right here in this special place. Will you marry me?'

Tears pricked Lucy's eyes. 'Oh Jake, there is nothing I would like more. Of course I will.' They were laughing and crying together when the sun, slipping away to the horizon, suddenly took on a radiant pink glow, the colour reflecting across the sea to the shore. 'Well, if that isn't affirmation from the heavens, I don't know what is!'

Acknowledgements

I would like to thank all those who have encouraged me to write a second novel, having read my first! Their confidence in my ability far outweighs my own, so thank you – you know who you are.

I want to give a special thank you, once again, to the amazing Helen Jarvis, who has continued to be my proof-reader, cover illustrator, deadline setter and marketing agent for one of my most prolific sellers - The George Hotel, South Molton. And thanks to Mark at The George for agreeing to stock my books.

Thanks also to Avril MacDonald, a longstanding school friend and self-appointed PR agent, who is on my case to bring the books to a greater readership. She is an expert in this field, which I most certainly am not, so her generous help is much appreciated.

Thanks must also go to Chella at Honeybee Books. She continues to guide me through the whole publishing process and to magically transform my manuscripts into actual books. Thank you for being so patient with me!

Part of the joy of writing *The Thin Place* was the opportunity it provided to revisit childhood haunts for research, particularly the coast between Loe Bar and St Michael's Mount, and the wonderful fishing village of Porthleven. Please forgive any liberties I have taken while weaving the story into this beautiful part of the world – it is all done with love for the county of Cornwall.

Lastly, thanks to my husband Blake, for continuing to believe in me and support my writing, even when I disappear for hours on end, only to reappear when he calls me for a cup of tea!

About the Author

Born into a Naval family, my childhood was spent moving every few years to a new area. We mainly lived in Devon and Cornwall but also Dorset, Hampshire, Scotland and the USA. Having attended seven schools by the age of ten, I went to boarding school on the edge of Dartmoor, to be nearer extended family and save my education!

I believe my affinity with Devon and Cornwall stems from a childhood spent in the area and historical family ties - my great grandfather was vicar of both Tintagel and Lelant churches.

After raising my family in Kent, towards the end of my 25-year career working as a PA in the NHS, I began writing. My youngest son challenged me to write a novel and, having been inspired by the real life 'Sea House', some seven years later it was published!

Now retired and living in North Devon with my husband, I have more time to devote to writing and have now completed my second novel.

BV - #0067 - 300924 - C0 - 210/148/12 - PB - 9781913675455 - Matt Lamination